THIS BOOK
BELONGS TO:

Mary C.

Imbimbo

CINDERELLA
AND OTHER CLASSIC ITALIAN FAIRY TALES

CHILDREN'S CLASSICS

This unique series of Children's Classics™ features accessible and highly readable texts paired with the work of talented and brilliant illustrators of bygone days to create fine editions for today's parents and children to rediscover and treasure. Besides being a handsome addition to any home library, this series features genuine bonded-leather spines stamped in gold, full-color illustrations, and high-quality acid-free paper that will enable these books to be passed from one generation to the next.

Adventures of Huckleberry Finn
The Adventures of Tom Sawyer
Aesop's Fables
Alice's Adventures in Wonderland
Andersen's Fairy Tales
Anne of Avonlea
Anne of Green Gables
At the Back of the North Wind
Black Beauty
The Call of the Wild
A Child's Book of Country Stories
A Child's Book of Stories
A Child's Book of Stories from
    Many Lands
A Child's Christmas
A Christmas Carol and Other
    Christmas Stories
Cinderella and Other Classic Italian
    Fairy Tales
The Complete Mother Goose
Great Dog Stories
Grimm's Fairy Tales
Hans Brinker *or* The Silver Skates
Heidi

The Hound of the Baskervilles
The Jungle Book
Just So Stories
Kidnapped
King Arthur and His Knights
A Little Child's Book of Stories
Little Men
The Little Princess
Little Women
Peter Pan
Rebecca of Sunnybrook Farm
Robin Hood
Robinson Crusoe
The Secret Garden
The Sleeping Beauty and Other
    Classic French Fairy Tales
The Swiss Family Robinson
Tales from Shakespeare
Through the Looking Glass and
    What Alice Found There
Treasure Island
A Very Little Child's Book of
    Stories
The Wind in the Willows

CINDERELLA
AND OTHER CLASSIC ITALIAN FAIRY TALES

Edited and with an Introduction by
Christine Messina

Drawings by Arthur Rackham
and Color Illustrations by
Warwick Goble

CHILDREN'S CLASSICS
New York • Avenel

This 1993 edition is published by Children's Classics, a division of dilithium Press, Ltd.,
distributed by Outlet Book Company, Inc., a Random House Company, 40 Engelhard
Avenue, Avenel, New Jersey 07001.

DILITHIUM is a registered trademark and CHILDREN'S CLASSICS is a trademark of
dilithium Press, Ltd.

Printed and bound in the United States of America

Library of Congress Cataloging-in-Publication Data

Cinderella and other classic Italian fairy tales / illustrated by Warwick Goble and Arthur
Rackham.
   p.   cm.
    Summary: An illustrated collection of traditional Italian fairy tales.
   ISBN 0–517–03707–6
   1. Fairy tales—Italy. [1. Fairy tales. 2. Folklore—Italy.] I. Goble, Warwick, ill.
II. Rackham, Arthur, 1867–1939, ill. III. Title: Cinderella.
   PZ8.C4894 1993
   [398.21'0945]—dc20   93–15523
                                                         CIP
                                                           AC

Cover design by Don Bender
Production supervision by Roméo Enriquez
Editorial supervision by Claire Booss and Gregory R. Suriano

Cover illustrations by Arthur Rackham

8 7 6 5 4 3 2 1

CONTENTS

Contents

LIST OF COLOR ILLUSTRATIONS

PREFACE TO
THIS ILLUSTRATED EDITION

THE STRIKING and witty silhouettes which decorate the front pages and the title story of this book were created by Arthur Rackham, one of England's finest watercolorists and foremost Edwardian book illustrators. Indeed, he has been described as "the lyric genius of the English people," and his work is revered today by those who appreciate and collect book illustration.

The stories have been beautifully brought to life in Warwick Goble's extraordinary paintings, where jewel-like colors enhance the scenes so that they truly can be called visions. (In addition, there are occasional line drawings throughout the text, by an unknown artist.)

Warwick Goble was best known for his expertise with watercolor and was also one of the premier book illustrators of the late nineteenth and early twentieth century. His art was greatly enriched by his early training at a painting firm, which gave him a superb understanding of color reproduction, and by his travels in the Orient, where he became fascinated by Asian art, an influence that can be plainly seen in his work.

Preface

Children's Classics is delighted to bring together the art of these fine illustrators, who worked during much the same period, in the same country, and in the same medium, but were not customarily published together, and never before in connection with these Italian tales.

CLAIRE BOOSS
Series Editor

INTRODUCTION

THE FIRST Cinderella story was probably told in China in the ninth century when people spoke of a girl named Yeh-hsien who was brought up by a wicked stepmother who ill-treated her and killed a fish that had befriended her. Over the centuries, nearly seven hundred different versions of Cinderella have been identified. One of them turned up in *Il Pentamerone*, or *The Five Days*, the stories collected here and the first European book to include a Cinderella tale. First published in 1637, these Italian stories were the first folk tales ever to appear in print, written down in the Neapolitan dialect by Giambattista Basile, who listened to old tales of enchantment and superstition told by Italian peasants living in and around Venice, Crete, and the Mediterranean coast. In editing these stories, I have used a collection based on John Edward Taylor's translation of 1847, but I have retold them for today's young readers.

In a thousand years, in hundreds of different versions, two themes have remained constant in all Cinderella stories: a young girl, through no fault of her own, has been demoted from her rightful place; to restore her to her former position, she is helped by a magical friend, often in the form of an

Introduction

animal or, in this Italian version, a date tree that was a gift from a good fairy. Metaphorically speaking—and Italian fairy tales are particularly rich in their metaphors—the helper represents the spirit of Cinderella's dead mother who comes back to help her despondent child. The picture of Cinderella sitting among the ashes is not a comment on her social standing, but a sign of her loneliness and despair.

Between these broad strokes, details vary enormously. As the tale was handed down from neighbor to neighbor and parent to child, bits of the story were altered to fit what was going on in the household or village on that particular day.

Basile's version of Cinderella is quite different from the French version by Perrault, published just sixty years later, on which modern versions of the tale have been based. The Italian version has nary a pumpkin nor a mouse in sight. And while a slipper figures in the final pages of the story, it is an ordinary cloth shoe.

What overwhelms and distinguishes the Italian version from all others is the powerful family drama that sets the story in motion: a father who once loved his daughter more than anyone in the world is tricked into turning his back on her. It is a theme that resonates for every child. Here the parent-child relationship takes precedence over the love story between Cinderella and the Prince. Happily, the father finally comes to his senses and renews his love for his child.

The themes of family love and loyalty cast a giant net over all the Italian fairy tales. A father may send his stupid or troublesome son alone into the world, but soon learns that the boy is really brave and wise. When the son returns home a rich man, his father repents. Sometimes, it is the child who is disloyal and ungrateful, as in the case of Little Goat-Face, a little peasant girl brought up like a princess by a giant lizard. After she has grown up rich and beautiful, she turns her back on her homely adoptive parent and suffers the consequences.

Within the symphonic themes of family loyalty are played many common tunes of life: ingratitude, envy, jealousy. The story of "Corvetto at the King's Court" could have happened today or in any age, as envious courtiers plot to destroy Corvetto because he is the King's favorite.

The Italians liked their stories to be entertaining and to depict real-life events, such as might happen to any family in Italy—that is, if someone in the family captured a pretty little flea in a bottle and it grew to be the size of a sheep! The Italian tales also tend to be more robust than other fairy tales, and easily mix the fabulous and the real: a poor woman who cannot have any children adopts a baby serpent and cares for him so well that he grows up into a great big serpent. (But, of course, he is really a prince!) Stories are set in real towns, and ogres belong to the logal ogres' guild, and ogresses have to put up with their in-laws just like everybody else.

In two important ways the Italian tales differ from German and French fairy tales: they are generally more humorous and considerably less cruel. Yes, there are some gory details—how else would you dispatch a dragon?—and certainly there is injustice. But the Italian tales touch on these crimes and hurry on. Nor does the storyteller waste any tears on the victims, whether innocent or guilty. The story moves swiftly on to a speedy conclusion in which virtue triumphs and evil is pun-

Introduction

ished. Often, to make the sentence easier to swallow, the evil-doer chooses his or her own punishment—being tossed into a dungeon, out the window, or onto the flames—and all ends well.

Most of the stories are episodic, and the narrative quickly moves from country to country, year to year, giving people plenty of room to grow and change, learn from their mistakes, and reclaim their fortunes.

Italian stories make few distinctions between dragons and ogres. Similarly, it's hard to say what a king might be. In some stories, a king and his court operate like real governments; and when a king must solve a problem—even if he is the Mouse King—he calls for the advice of his councillors. But in most of the stories, a king is simply a "gentleman," without any royal court to speak of. One king may live next door to another, and an ogress may live across the street.

The threads of love run through every story, but these are no ordinary love stories. Here are tales of forbidden love between two incompatible worlds. Spells are cast to make one lover forget another. Will he—or she—remain true to the loved one? Princes change form as rapidly as you change your socks—from a slave to a serpent to a dove. Will the princess still love him and recognize him underneath the scales or the feathers? Will the prince recognize *her*, although she is dressed in rags? The hero and heroine must demonstrate faithfulness and perseverance before everything can come out right in the end.

Marriage is the final triumph, because in Italy marriage is the ultimate goal of life. Daughters are marriage prizes, yet

Introduction

daughters, and women in general, have a remarkable amount of freedom and influence, considering the time at which these tales were written. Girls are enterprising and courageous, saving their lovers by their own wits. The beautiful Filadoro, in "Filadoro and the Dove," for example, helps her enslaved prince escape, and when he forgets all about her, she takes her fate into her own hands to regain his love. Even female animals wield an astonishing amount of power. The cat in "Pippo and The Clever Cat" makes a rich man out of a pauper, and in the end is betrayed for all her pains.

Repeatedly in these stories, the females stride fearlessly into dangerous territory to recover their lost loves. However, these are Italian stories, and sooner or later girls and boys alike always make their peace with their fathers and mothers.

While there is almost always a king and almost always a prince and princess, these tales also portray the lives of ordinary working people, and the point of departure of many stories is spurred by hunger or unemployment: these are the springboards into wonderland. Although princes may be transformed into serpents, and a princess's robes into rags, all things marvelous and fabulous grow out of real longings and real deeds. The magic powers of heroes or heroines merely complement their natural strength and persistence. Fantasy may intercede to help move things along—much like a winning lottery ticket today could change a poor man's hut into a palace. But while the lottery winner doesn't need to have a good character, in these tales only a good heart can alter fate and bring good fortune.

CHRISTINE MESSINA

CINDERELLA
AND OTHER CLASSIC ITALIAN FAIRY TALES

CINDERELLA

THERE once lived a Prince, who was a widower. He had an only daughter, so dear to him that he saw everything through her eyes. He kept a governess for her, who taught her crocheting and knitting and lace making, and showed her much affection. But the Princess was very lonely, and many a time she said to the governess, "Oh, that you were my mother, you who show me such kindness and love." She said this so often that, at last, the governess said to her one day, "If you will do as this foolish head of mine advises I shall be mother to you, and you will be as dear to me as the apple of my eye."

She was going to say more, when Zezolla, for that was the name of the Princess, said, "Pardon me if I stop you. I know you wish me well. Therefore, say no more. Only show me the way. If you write, I will subscribe." "Well, then," answered the governess, "open your ears and listen, and you will have bread as white as the flowers. You know that your father would do anything to please you. Entreat him when he is caressing you to marry me and make me Princess. Then, bless your stars! You shall be the mistress of my life."

When Zezolla heard this, the hours seemed to drag until she could do all that her governess had advised. As soon as the mourning for her mother's death ended, she began to beg her father to marry the governess. At first, the Prince took it as a joke. But Zezolla kept trying until at last he gave way to her entreaties. He married the governess and gave a great feast at the wedding.

Now, while the young folks were dancing, and Zezolla was standing at the window of her house, a dove came flying and perched upon a wall, saying to her, "Whenever you need anything send the request to the Dove of the Fairies in the Island of Sardinia, and you will instantly have what you wish."

For five or six days the new stepmother overwhelmed Zezolla with caresses, seating her at the best place at table, giving her the choicest morsels to eat, and clothing her in the richest apparel. But soon, forgetting entirely the good service she had received, she began to bring six daughters of her own into the house. She had never before told anyone that she was a widow with a bunch of girls. She praised them so much, and talked to her husband in such a fashion, that at last the stepdaughters had all his favor, and he forgot all about his own child. In short, it fared so ill with the poor girl, bad today and worse tomorrow, that she was moved out of the royal chamber into the kitchen, from the canopy of state to the hearth, from splendid apparel of silks and gold to dishcloths and rags. All day long, from sunup to dark, and half the night, too, she worked in the kitchen, washing the laundry and sweeping the hearth until it was clean even of one cinder; and she waited upon the stepsisters and her stepmother like a servant. Her face grew pale and her hair hung down so straight around her shoulders that she no longer even looked the same. Not only was her condition changed, but even her name. For, instead of Zezolla,

All day long Cinderella worked in the kitchen, washing the laundry
and sweeping the hearth.

she was now called Cinderella, for at the end of her work she would go and sit among the ashes.

It happened that the Prince had occasion to go to Sardinia upon affairs of state. Calling the six stepdaughters, he asked them, one by one, what they would like him to bring them on his return. One wished for splendid dresses, another to have ornaments for her hair, another rouge for her face, another asked for toys and trinkets: one wished for this and one for that. At last the Prince said to his own daughter, mocking her, "And what would you have, my child?"

"Nothing, Father," she replied, "but that you remember me to the Dove of the Fairies, and bid her send me something. If you forget my request, may you be unable to move backwards or forwards. Remember what I ask."

The Prince went on his way and did his business in Sardinia, and purchased all the items that his stepdaughters had asked for. But he forgot all about poor Cinderella. On board ship he set sail to return, but the ship could not get out of the harbor. It was stuck there, held fast. The captain of the ship was in despair and fairly tired out. He laid himself down to sleep, and in his dream he saw a fairy, who said to him, "Do you know the reason why you cannot sail the ship out of port? It is because the Prince has broken his promise to his daughter, remembering everyone except his own child."

When the captain awoke he told his dream to the Prince, who, in shame and confusion, went at once to the Grotto of the Fairies, and, remembering his daughter to them, asked them to send her something. Behold, there stepped forth from the grotto a beautiful maiden, who thanked his daughter for

Cinderella

her kind remembrances, and bade him tell her to be merry and of good heart. And then she gave him a date tree, a hoe, and a little bucket made of gold, and a silken napkin.

The Prince, marvelling at this present, took leave of the fairy, and returned to his own country. When he had given his stepdaughters all the presents they had desired, he at last gave his own daughter the gift which the fairy had sent her. Overjoyed, Cinderella took the date tree and planted it in a pretty flowerpot, hoed the earth around it, watered it from the golden bucket, and wiped its leaves morning and evening with the silken napkin. In a few days the tree had grown as tall as a woman, and out of it came a fairy, who said to Cinderella, "What do you wish for?" And Cinderella replied that she wished sometimes to leave the house without her sisters' knowledge. The fairy answered, "Whenever you desire this, come to the flowerpot and say:

> *My little date tree, my golden tree,*
> *With a golden hoe I have hoed thee,*
> *With a golden can I have watered thee,*
> *With a silken cloth I have wiped thee dry,*
> *Now strip thee and dress me speedily.''*

When the time for a great feast at the palace arrived, the stepmother's daughters appeared, dressed up so fine, all ribbons and flowers, and slippers and shoes, sweet smells and bells, and roses and posies. Cinderella ran quickly to the flowerpot, and no sooner had she repeated the fairy's words, than she was dressed like a queen, seated upon a beautiful horse, and attended by twelve smart pages, all in their best clothes. Then she went to the ball, and the sisters were envious of this unknown beauty whom they didn't recognize.

Even the young King himself was there, and as soon as he saw Cinderella he stood spellbound with amazement, and ordered a trusted servant to find out the name of the beautiful maiden and where she lived. The servant followed her horse but when Cinderella noticed him she threw on the ground a handful of gold coins which the fairy had given her for this purpose. The servant lighted his lantern and was so busy picking up all the coins that he forgot to follow the horse. Cinderella came home quite safely, and had changed her clothes, as the fairy told her. When the wicked sisters arrived home, to vex her and make her envious, they told her of all the fine things they had seen.

The King was very angry with the servant, and warned him not to miss finding out next time who this beautiful maiden was, and where she lived.

Soon there was another feast, and again the sisters all went to it, leaving poor Cinderella at home on the kitchen hearth. She ran quickly to the date tree, and repeated the spell, and instantly there appeared a number of damsels, one with a looking-glass, another with a bottle of rose water, another with curling irons, another with combs, another with pins, another with dresses, and another with capes and collars. They decked her out as glorious as the sun, and put her in a coach drawn by six white horses, and attended by footmen and pages in livery. No sooner did Cinderella appear in the ballroom than the

No sooner did Cinderella appear in the ballroom than the King was overcome
with love.

hearts of the sisters were filled with amazement, and the King was overcome with love.

When Cinderella went home that night the servant followed her again, but she threw down a handful of pearls and jewels, and the good fellow, seeing how valuable they were, stopped to pick them up. So again she had time to slip away home and take off her fine dress as before.

The servant returned slowly to the King, who cried out when he saw him, "By the souls of my ancestors, if you do not find out who she is you shall have such a thrashing and as many kicks as you have hairs in your beard!"

When the next feast was held, and the sisters were safely out of the house, Cinderella went to the date tree, and once again repeated the spell. In an instant, she found herself splendidly arrayed and seated in a coach of gold, with ever so many servants around her, so that she looked just like a queen. Again, the sisters were beside themselves with envy. This time, when she left the palace after the ball, the King's servant ran alongside the coach. Cinderella, seeing that he was ever running by her side, cried, "Coachman, drive on quickly." The coach set off at such a rattling pace that she lost one of her slippers, the prettiest thing that ever was seen. The servant, unable to catch the coach, which flew like a bird, picked up the slipper and carried it to the King. Whereupon the King, taking the slipper in his hand, said, "If the basement, indeed, is so beautiful, what must the building be. You who held a white foot now enclose my unhappy heart!"

Then the king proclaimed that all the women in the country should come to a banquet, for which the most splendid

When she left the palace after the ball, Cinderella lost
one of her slippers.

provision was made of pies and pastries, and stews and ragouts and sweetmeats—enough to feed a whole army. And when all the women were assembled, nobles and peasants, rich and poor, beautiful and ugly, the King tried the slipper on each one of the guests to see whom it should fit to a hair. But not one foot could he find to fit it. He looked carefully at all the guests to make sure everyone in the kingdom was there. The Prince confessed that he had left one daughter behind. "But," said he, "she is always on the hearth, and is such a graceless simpleton that she is unworthy to sit and eat at your table." The King said, "Tomorrow I will give another feast and she shall be the very first on the list."

So all the guests departed. The next day they assembled again, and with the wicked sisters came Cinderella. When the King saw her he had his suspicions, but said nothing. After the feast came the trial of the slipper. As soon as it approached Cinderella's foot, it darted on to it of its own accord like iron flies to the magnet. Seeing this, the King took her in his arms, and, seating her under the royal canopy, he set the crown upon her head, whereupon all bowed and paid homage to her as their queen.

When the wicked sisters saw this they were full of venom and rage and, not having patience to look upon the object of their hatred, they slipped quietly away on tiptoe and went home to their mother, confessing, in spite of themselves, that—

He is mad who resists Fate.

THE MAID IN THE MYRTLE TREE

THERE lived in the village of Miano a man and his wife who had no children whatever, and they longed with the greatest eagerness to have an heir. The woman was forever saying, "O Heavens! If I could only have a little baby— I should not care, were it even a sprig of a myrtle." She repeated this song so often, and so wearied Heaven with her words, that at last her wish was granted, and at the end of nine months, instead of a little boy or girl, she placed in the hands of the nurse a fine sprig of myrtle. The new mother planted the sprig with great delight in a pot, ornamented with many beautiful figures, and set it in the window, tending it morning and evening with more care than the gardener does a bed of cabbages from which he hopes to pay the rent for his garden.

Now the King's son happening to pass by on his way to a hunt, took a fancy to this beautiful plant, and asked the mistress of the house if she would sell it. He said that he liked it so much that he would even give one of his eyes for it. The woman at last, after a thousand refusals, lured by his offers, dazzled by his promises, frightened by his threats and, finally, overcome by his prayers, gave him the pot, begging him to hold it dear, for she loved it more than a daughter, and valued it as much as if it were her own child. The Prince had the flowerpot carried with the greatest care into his own rooms,

11

and placed it on a balcony, where he tended and watered it with his own hand.

It happened one evening, when the Prince had gone to bed, and all were asleep in the castle that he heard the sound of someone stealing through the chamber and coming cautiously towards his bed. He thought it must be some chamberboy coming to steal a few pennies from his purse, or some mischievous imp to pull the bedcovers off him. But as he was a bold fellow, whom none could frighten, he played dead, and waited to see what would happen. When he sensed the creature coming nearer, he stretched out his hand into the darkness. Instead of laying hold, as he expected, to the prickles of a hedgehog, he touched a little maiden more soft and fine than merino wool, more pliant and tender than a marten's tail, more delicate than thistledown. His mind flew from one thought to another, and taking her to be a fairy (as indeed she was), he felt at once a great affection for her. But the next morning, before the sun rose, the unknown fair one disappeared, leaving the Prince filled with curiosity and wonder.

The next night she returned once more to his room, and left again with the dawn. When this had gone on for seven days, the Prince was burning and melting with desire to know what good fortune this was that the stars had showered down on him. So one night, when the fair maiden was fast asleep, he tied one of her tresses to his arm, that she might not escape. Then he called a servant and, bidding him light the candles, he saw the flower of beauty, the miracle of women, a beautiful dove, he saw a golden trinket, a moon in the fifteenth day, a jewel fit for a king.

The Maid in the Myrtle Tree

In astonishment he cried, "O sleep, sweet sleep! Heap poppies on the eyes of this lovely jewel. Do not interrupt my delight in viewing as long as I can this triumph of beauty. O lovely tress that binds me! O lovely eyes that inflame me! O lovely lips that refresh me! Oh, where was this living statue made?"

So saying he made a circle of his arms, and as he clasped her neck, she awoke from her sleep and replied with a gentle smile to the sigh of the enamored Prince. Seeing her open her eyes, he said, "O my treasure, if I loved you in the darkness, what will become of my life now that I have seen you in the candlelight? O beauteous eyes, you alone have pierced this heart! O my lovely physician, take pity on one who is sick with love; who is seized by a fever. Lay your hand on this heart, feel my pulse, and give me a prescription. But, my soul, why do I ask for medicine? I desire no other comfort than a touch of that little hand, for I am certain that with the healing sound of your voice, I shall be well again."

At these words the lovely fairy grew as red as fire and replied, "Not so much praise, my lord Prince! I am your servant, and would do anything in the world to serve that kingly face, and I esteem it great good fortune that from a bunch of myrtle, set in a pot of earth, I have become a branch of laurel hung over the door of a heart in which there is so much greatness and virtue."

The Prince, melting at these words, began again to embrace her. He gave her his hand, saying, "Take my faith, you shall be my wife, you shall have the key to this heart, as you hold the helm of this life." He sealed his promise with a kiss.

13

The Maid in the Myrtle Tree

After a hundred other ceremonies and discourses, they exchanged private vows, and the fairy maid promised to live only in the Prince's chamber.

But Fate is always a hindrance to the steps of Love. It happened that the Prince was called by his father to hunt a great wild boar which was ravaging the country. So he was forced to leave his wife. But as he loved her more than his life, and knew that she was beautiful beyond all beautiful things, there sprang up the feeling of jealousy, which is a tempest in the sea of love, making life always restless, the mind unstable, the heart ever suspicious. So, calling his fairy wife, he said to her, "I am obliged, my heart, to be away from home for two or three days. Heaven knows with how much grief I tear myself from you, who are my soul, and Heaven knows too whether my life may not end; but as I cannot help going, to please my father, I must leave you. I, therefore, pray you, by all the love you bear me, to go back into the flowerpot, and not to come out of it till I return, which will be as soon as possible."

"I will do so," said the fairy, "for I cannot refuse what pleases you. Go, therefore, and may the mother of good luck go with you, for I will serve you to the best of my power. But do me one favor. Leave a thread of silk with a bell tied to the top of the myrtle, and when you come back pull the thread and ring, and immediately I will come out and say, 'Here I am.'"

The Prince did so, and then calling his most trusted attendant, said to him, "Come hither and open your ears. Make this bed every evening, as if I were myself to sleep in it. Water this flowerpot regularly. Mind, I have counted the leaves, and if I

14

find one missing I will fire you at once." So saying, he mounted his horse, and went, like a sheep that is led to the slaughter, to follow a boar. In the meantime seven wicked women, with whom the Prince had been acquainted, began to grow jealous; and being curious to learn his secret, they sent for a mason, and for a good sum of money got him to make an underground passage from their house into the Prince's chamber. Then these cunning witches went through the passage in order to explore. Finding the room empty, they opened the window, and when they saw the beautiful myrtle standing there, each of them plucked a leaf from it. But the youngest took off the entire top, to which the little bell was hung. The moment it was touched, the bell tinkled and the fairy, thinking it was the Prince, immediately came out.

As soon as the wicked women saw this lovely creature they fastened their talons on her, crying, "It is you who have stolen the heart of the Prince! But you come to an end of your tricks, my fine lady! You are nimble enough in running off, but you are caught in your tricks this time, and if you escape, it will be as if you were never born."

So saying, they flew upon her, and instantly tore her to pieces, and each of them took a part. But the youngest would not join in this cruel act. When she was invited by her sisters to do as they did, she would take nothing but a lock of golden hair. When they had done they went quickly away by the passage through which they had come.

Meanwhile, the attendant came to make the bed and water the flowerpot, according to his master's orders, and seeing this pretty piece of work, he almost died of terror. Then, biting his nails with vexation, he gathered up the remains of the flesh and bones that were left, and, scraping the blood from the floor, he piled them all up in a heap in the pot. Having watered it, he made the bed, locked the door, put the key under the door and, taking to his heels, ran out of the town.

When the Prince came back from the chase, he went straight to the chamber and, not having patience to call the attendant and ask for the key, he gave the lock a kick and burst open the door. He went in, opened the window, and seeing the myrtle stripped of its leaves, he fell to making the most doleful lamentation, crying, shouting, and bawling, "O wretched me! Unhappy me! O miserable me! Who has played me this trick? O ruined, banished, and undone prince! O my leafless myrtle! My lost fairy! O my wretched life, my joys vanished into smoke, my pleasures turned to vinegar! What will you do, unhappy man? You have fallen from all happiness. You are robbed of every treasure! You are expelled from life, and do you not go mad? Where are you? Where are you, my myrtle? And what soul more hard than marble has destroyed this beautiful flowerpot? O cursed chase, that has chased me from all happiness! Alas! I am done for, I am overthrown, I am ruined, I have ended my days. It is not possible for me to get through life without my life. Without my love sleep will be lamentation, food poison, pleasure insipid, and life sour."

These and many other exclamations that would move the very stones in the streets, were uttered by the Prince. After repeating them again and again, and wailing bitterly, full of sorrow and woe, never closing his eyes to sleep, nor opening his mouth to eat, he gave way totally to grief.

The Maid in the Myrtle Tree

In the meantime, the fairy had sprouted up again from the remains that were put in the pot. Seeing the misery of her poor lover, and how he was turned in a second to the color of a sick person, she was moved with compassion and, springing out of the pot, she stood before him. Embracing him, she said, "Take heart, take heart, my Prince! Have done now with this lamenting, wipe your eyes, quiet your anger, smooth your face. Behold me alive and well, in spite of those wicked women who split my head and so ill-treated me."

The Prince, seeing this when he least expected it, arose again from death to life, and the color returned to his cheeks, warmth to his blood, breath to his breast. After giving her a thousand caresses and embraces, he desired to know the whole affair; and when he found that the attendant was not to blame, he ordered him to be called home. Then, with the full consent of his father, the Prince gave a lavish banquet and before all of the great people in his kingdom he married the fairy again. Of all of the people invited to the banquet, the Prince wished to have present those seven wicked women who had committed the slaughter of that sweet maiden.

As soon as they had done eating, the Prince asked all the guests, one after another, what he deserved who had injured that beautiful maiden—pointing to the fairy, who looked so lovely that she captured hearts like a sprite and gathered souls to her like a windmill.

Then all who sat at the table, beginning with the King, replied. One said that he deserved the gallows; another, that he merited the whip; a third, to be thrown from a clifftop. In short, one proposed this punishment and another that. At last, it came to the turn of the seven wicked women to speak. Although they did not much relish this conversation, wine had loosened their tongues and they answered that whoever had the heart to even touch this beauty deserved to be buried alive in a dungeon.

"As you have pronounced this sentence with your own lips," said the Prince, "you have chosen your own fate. I will cause your order to be executed, since it is you who made a fritter of this beautiful head and chopped off these lovely limbs. So quick, make haste, lose not a moment! Throw them this very instant into a large dungeon, where they shall end their days miserably."

So, this order was instantly carried out. But the Prince spared the youngest sister of these wicked witches and married her to the attendant and gave her a good dowry. He also gave the father and mother of the myrtle enough fortune to live comfortably, while he himself spent his days happily with the fairy. And while the wicked women ended their lives in bitter anguish. All of this demonstrated the truth of the old proverb—

*Even a lame goat can hop over the highest fences
with a little help.*

PERUONTO THE FOOL

ONCE upon a time a woman who lived in a village, and was called Ceccarella, had a son named Peruonto, who was one of the most stupid lads that ever was born. This made his mother very unhappy, and all day long she grieved because of this great misfortune. For whether she asked him kindly, or stormed at him till her throat was dry, the foolish fellow would not stir to do the slightest hand's turn for her. At last, after a thousand dinnings at his brain, and saying "I tell you" and "I told you" day after day, she got him to go to the woods for a bundle of wood, saying, "Come now, it is time for us to eat, so run off for some sticks, and don't forget yourself on the way, but come back as quick as you can, and we will boil ourselves some cabbage, to keep the life in us."

Away went the stupid Peruonto, hanging his head as if he were going to jail. Away he went, counting his steps, at the pace of a snail's crawl, and making all sorts of zigzags and excursions on his way to the woods. And when he reached the middle of a plain, through which ran a river, he saw three youths who had made themselves a bed of grass and a pillow of a great flint stone, and were lying sound asleep under the blaze of the Sun, who was shooting his rays down on them point blank. When Peruonto saw these poor creatures, looking as if they were in the midst of a fountain of fire, he felt pity for

19

them, and, cutting some branches of oak, he made a handsome arbor over them. Meanwhile the youths, who were the sons of a fairy, awoke, and, seeing the kindness and courtesy of Peruonto, they gave him a charm, saying that every thing he asked for would be done.

Peruonto, having performed this good action, went on his ways towards the woods where he made up such an enormous bundle of wood that it would have needed an engine to draw it. Seeing that he could not in any way get it on his back, he sat astride it and cried, "Oh, what a lucky fellow I would be if this bundle would carry me riding on horseback!" The words were hardly out of his mouth when the bundle began to trot and gallop like a great horse, and when it came to the front of the King's palace, it pranced and capered in a way that would amaze you. On seeing such a wonderful sight, the ladies who were standing at one of the windows ran to call Vastolla, the daughter of the King. When she saw the bounding bundle of wood, she burst out laughing—a thing which, owing to a natural melancholy, she was never known to have done before. Peruonto raised his head, and, seeing that it was at him that she was laughing, exclaimed, "Oh, Vastolla, I wish that I could be your husband and I would soon cure you of laughing at me!" And so saying, he struck his heels into the bundle, and in a dashing gallop he was quickly at home, with such a train of little boys at his heels that if his mother had not been quick to shut the door they would soon have killed him with the stones and sticks with which they pelted him.

Now Vastolla's father wished to marry her to some great prince, and he invited all he knew to come and visit him and

pay their respects to the Princess. But she refused to have anything to say to any of them, and only answered, "I will marry
only the young man who rode on the bundle." The King got
more and more angry with every refusal, and at last he was
quite unable to contain himself any longer. He called his council together, saying, "You know by this time how my honor
has been shamed, and that my daughter has acted in such a
manner that my reputation is ruined. Now speak and advise
me. I say that she is unworthy to live, seeing that she has
brought on me such discredit, and I wish to do away with her
before she does more mischief."

The councillors, who had in their time learned much wisdom, said, "In truth, she deserves to be severely punished. But,
after all, it is this audacious scoundrel who has given you the
annoyance, and it is not right that he should escape punishment. Let us wait till he comes to light. When we discover the
root of this disgrace, then we will think it over and decide
what is best to be done." This counsel pleased the King, for he
saw that they spoke like sensible, prudent men. He held up his
hand and said, "We will wait and see the end of this business."

The King held a great banquet, and invited every one of
his nobles and all the gentlemen in his kingdom to come to it.
Vastolla sat at the high table at the top of the hall. The King
said, "When she recognizes the fellow, we shall see her eyes
turn to him, and we will instantly lay hold of him and put him
away." But when the feasting was done, and all the guests
passed out in a line, Vastolla took no notice of them. The King
grew more angry than ever, and vowed that he would kill her
without more delay. Again, however, the councillors pacified

him and said, "Softly, softly, Your Majesty! Quiet your wrath. Let us have another banquet tomorrow, not for noblemen, but for the lower sort. Some women always attach themselves to the worst, and we shall find among the cutlers, and bead-makers, and comb-sellers, the root of your anger, which we have not discovered among the cavaliers."

The King fancied this idea and he ordered a second banquet, this time inviting all the riffraff and ragtag of the city, such as rogues, scavengers, tinkers, pedlars, sweeps, beggars, and such rabble, who were all in high glee. Taking their seats like noblemen at a great long table, they began to feast and gobble away.

Now, when Peruonto's mother heard this invitation, she urged her son to go, until at last she got him to set out for the feast. Scarcely had he arrived there when Vastolla cried out without thinking, "That is my Knight of the Bundle." When the King heard this he tore his beard, seeing his prize had fallen to an ugly lout, the very sight of whom he could not endure, with a shaggy head, owl's eyes, a parrot's nose, a deer's mouth, and legs bare and bandy. Heaving a deep sigh, he said, "What can that daughter of mine have seen to make her take a fancy to this ogre, or strike up a dance with this hairy-foot? Ah, vile, false creature, who has cast so base a spell on her? But why do we wait? Let her suffer the punishment she deserves. Take her from my presence, for I cannot bear to look longer upon her."

The councillors consulted together and resolved that Vastolla, as well as Peruonto, should be shut up in a cask and thrown into the sea. So that the King would not have to stain his hands with the blood of one of his family, the councillors

carried out the sentence. No sooner was the judgment pronounced, than the cask was brought and both were put into it;
but before they sealed it, some of Vastolla's ladies, crying and
sobbing as if their hearts would break, put into it a basket of
raisins and dried figs that she might have a little food to live on
for a while. And when the cask was closed up, it was flung into
the sea, on which it went floating as the wind drove it.

Meanwhile, Vastolla, weeping till her eyes ran like two riv-
ers, said to Peruonto, "What a sad misfortune is this! Oh, if I
but knew who has played me this trick, to have me caged in
this dungeon! Alas, alas, to find myself in this plight without
knowing how. Tell me, tell me, O cruel man, what spell did
you use to bring me within the circle of this cask?" Peruonto
at last said, "If you want me to tell you, you must give me
some figs and raisins." So Vastolla, to draw the secret out of
him, gave him a handful of both; and as soon as he had eaten
them, he told her truly all that had befallen him—about the
three youths, and the bundle of wood that pranced like a horse,
and about herself standing at the window. When the poor lady
heard, she took heart and said to Peruonto, "My friend, shall
we then let our lives run out in a cask? Why don't you change
this tub into a fine ship and run into some good harbor?" And
Peruonto replied—

> "If you would have me say the spell,
> With figs and raisins feed me well!"

So Vastolla, to make him open his mouth, filled it with fruit;
and so she fished the words out of him. And lo! As soon as

23

Peruonto the Fool

Peruonto had said her wish the cask was turned into a beautiful ship, with sails and sailors and everything that could be wished for, and guns and trumpets and a splendid cabin in which Vastolla sat, filled with delight.

It being now the hour when the Moon begins to play seesaw with the Sun, Vastolla said to Peruonto, "My fine lad, now change this ship into a palace, for then we shall be more secure; you know the saying, 'Praise the Sea, but keep to the Land.'" And Peruonto replied—

> *"If you would have me say the spell,*
> *With figs and raisins feed me well!"*

So Vastolla fed him again, and Peruonto, swallowing the raisins and figs, did her pleasure; and immediately the ship came ashore and was changed into a beautiful palace, fitted up in a most sumptuous manner, and so full of furniture and curtains and hangings that there was nothing more to ask for. Vastolla, who, a little before, would not have given a penny for her chances, now did not wish to change places with the greatest lady in the world. To put the seal to all her good fortune, she begged Peruonto to turn himself into a handsome prince; for though the saying goes, "Better to have a pig for a husband, than only a smile from an emperor," still, if his appearance were changed, she should be the happiest woman in the universe. And Peruonto replied as before—

> *"If you would have me say the spell,*
> *With figs and raisins feed me well!"*

24

Then Vastolla quickly opened his lips, and scarcely had he spoken her wish aloud, when he was changed, as if from an owl to a nightingale, from an ogre to a beautiful youth, and from a scarecrow to a fine gentleman. Vastolla, seeing such a transformation, clasped him in her arms and was almost beside herself with joy. Then they were married and lived happily for years.

Meanwhile, the King grew old and very sad. One day, the courtiers persuaded him to go hunting, to cheer him up. Night overtook him, and, seeing a light in a palace, he sent a servant to ask if he could rest there. The answer came back that everything was at his disposal. The King went to the palace and passing into a great guest chamber, he saw only two little boys, who skipped around him crying, "Welcome, welcome!" The astonished King was enchanted, and sitting down to rest himself at a table, to his amazement he saw appear a richly embroidered tablecloth, with dishes full of roast meats and many sorts of foods. In truth, he feasted like a king, waited on by those beautiful children. All the while he sat at the table, a concert of lutes and tambourines never ceased—such delicious music that he tapped the tips of his fingers and toes. When he had done eating, a bed appeared all made of gold and having his boots taken off, he quickly fell asleep. All his courtiers did the same, after having fed heartily at a hundred tables, which were laid out in the other rooms.

When morning came, the King wished to thank the two little children, but with them appeared Vastolla and her husband. Embracing her father, she told him the whole story. The King, seeing that he had found two grandsons who were two jewels and a son-in-law who had magical powers, embraced first one and then the other. Taking up the children in his arms, he and they all returned to the city where there was a great festival that lasted many days, proving without doubt that—

A good deed is never lost.

VARDIELLO AND THE SILENT MAN

GRANNONIA of Aprano was a woman of great sense and judgment, but she had a son named Vardiello, who was the greatest booby in the whole country. Nevertheless, as a mother's eyes are bewitched and see what does not exist, she doted upon him so much that she was forever showering him with attention as if he were the handsomest boy in the world.

Now, Grannonia kept a hen, sitting upon a nest of eggs, in which she placed all her hope, expecting to have a fine brood of chickens, and to make a good profit from them. Having one day to go out on some business, she called her son and said to him, "My pretty son, listen to what I say: keep your eye upon the hen, and if she should get up to scratch and pick, look sharp and drive her back to the nest; otherwise her eggs will grow cold, and then we shall have neither eggs nor chickens."

"Leave it to me," replied Vardiello. "You are not speaking to deaf ears."

"One thing more," said the mother. "In yon cupboard is a pot full of certain poisonous nuts; take care that the Devil does not tempt you to touch them, for they would make you fall down dead in a minute."

"Heaven forbid!" replied Vardiello. "Poison indeed will

not tempt me. But you are wise to warn me; for if I had got at it, I should certainly have eaten it all up."

Thereupon the mother went out, while Vardiello stayed behind. He went into the garden to dig holes, which he covered with boughs, to catch the little thieves who come to steal the fruit. As he was working he saw the hen come running out of the room, whereupon he began to cry, "Hish, hish! This way, that way!" But the hen did not stir a foot. Vardiello, seeing that she had something of the donkey in her, began to stamp with his feet; and after stamping with his feet he threw his cap at her, and after the cap, a club which hit her upon the head, and made her quickly fall down dead.

When Vardiello saw this sad accident, he wondered how to remedy the evil. Making a virtue of necessity, to prevent the eggs growing cold, he sat himself down upon the nest. As he sat, he gave the eggs an unlucky blow, and quickly made an omelet of them. In despair at what he had done, he began to knock his head against the wall. At last, however, as all grief turns to hunger, his stomach began to grumble. Vardiello decided to eat the hen. He plucked her feathers, and stuck her upon a spit, then he made a great fire, and began to roast her. And when she was cooked, Vardiello, spread a clean cloth upon an old chest, and then, taking a jar, he went down into the cellar to draw some wine. Just as he was in the midst of drawing the wine, he heard an uproar in the house, which seemed like the clattering of horses' hoofs. Starting upstairs in alarm, he saw a big tomcat running off with the hen, spit and all, with another cat chasing after him, crying out for a part.

Vardiello darted after the cat like a lion, and in his haste left the tap of the wine barrel running. After chasing the cat through every hole and corner of the house, he recovered the hen, but the cask had meanwhile all run out. When Vardiello returned and saw the wine running all over the floor, he let the cask of his soul empty itself through the tap-holes of his eyes. But at last good sense came to his aid and he hit upon a plan to remedy the mischief, and prevent his mother's finding out what had happened. Taking a sack of flour, filled full to the brim, he sprinkled it over the wine on the floor.

But when he reckoned up on his fingers all the disasters he had met with, and all the fooleries he had committed, he thought his mother could never forgive him. He resolved in his heart not to let his mother see him again alive. So thrusting his hand into the jar of pickled walnuts, which his mother had said contained poison, he never stopped eating until he came to the bottom. When he had filled his stomach, he went and hid himself in the oven.

In the meanwhile, his mother returned, and stood knocking for a long time at the door. At last, seeing that no one came, she gave it a kick and, going in, she called her son at the top of her voice. But nobody answered. She imagined that some mischief must have happened, and she went on crying louder and louder, "Vardiello! Vardiello! Are you deaf, that you don't hear? Have you a cramp, that you don't run? Have you the fever, that you don't answer? Where are you, you rogue? Where are you hidden, you naughty fellow?"

Vardiello, on hearing all this hubbub, cried out at last with a piteous voice, "Here I am! Here I am in the oven. But you will never see me again, Mother!"

Vardiello and the Silent Man

"Why so?" said the poor mother.

"Because I am poisoned," replied the son.

"Alas! Alas!" cried Grannonia, "How came you to do that? Who has given you poison?"

Then Vardiello told her, one after another, all the pretty things he had done. On this account, he said, he wished to die and not to remain any longer a laughingstock in the world.

The poor woman, on hearing all this, was miserable and wretched. To drive this melancholy whimsy out of his head, she soothed and pampered him. Being dotingly fond of him, she gave him some nice sweetmeats, and convinced him that the pickled walnuts were not poison, but good and comforting to the stomach. Having thus pacified him with cheering words, and showered on him a thousand caresses, she drew him out of the oven. Then giving him a fine piece of cloth, she bade him go and sell it, but cautioned him not to do business with folks of too many words.

"Tut, tut!" said Vardiello, "Let me alone; I know what I'm about, never fear." So saying, he took the cloth, and went out through the city of Naples, crying, "Cloth! Cloth!" But whenever anyone asked him, "What cloth have you there?" he replied, "You are no customer for me; you are a man of too many words." And when another said to him, "How do you sell your cloth?" he called him a chatterbox, who deafened him with his noise. At length he chanced to see, in the deserted courtyard of a house, a plaster statue. Being tired out, and wearied with going about and about, he sat himself down on a bench. But not seeing anyone astir in the house, which looked

Vardiello and the Silent Man

abandoned, he said to the statue, "Tell me, comrade, does no one live in this house?" As the statue gave no answer, he thought this surely was a man of few words. So he said, "Friend, will you buy my cloth? I'll sell it you cheap." Seeing that the statue still remained dumb, he exclaimed, "I've found my man at last! There, take the cloth, examine it, and give me what you will. Tomorrow I'll return for the money."

So saying, Vardiello left the cloth on the spot where he had been sitting, and the first person who passed that way found the prize and carried it off.

When Vardiello returned home and told his mother all that had happened, she said to him, "When will you put that head of yours in order? See now what tricks you have played me! But I am myself to blame, for being too tenderhearted, instead of giving you a good beating. You'll go on with your pranks until one day we will come to a serious falling out, and then there will be a sad reckoning, my lad!"

"Softly, Mother," replied Vardiello. "Things are not so bad as they seem. Do you think me a fool, and that I don't know what I am about? Tomorrow is not yet here. Wait awhile, and you shall see whether I know how to do a good job."

The next morning, as soon as the shades of night had fled the country, Vardiello returned to the courtyard where the statue stood, and said, "Good day, friend! Can you give me those few pence you owe me? Come, quick, pay me for the cloth!" But when he saw that the statue remained speechless, he took up a stone and hurled it at its breast with such force that it burst a vein. Indeed, his troubles were over, for some pieces of the statue fell off, and underneath Vardiello discovered a pot full of golden coins. Taking the pot in both his hands, off he ran home, head over heels, as fast as he could scamper, crying out, "Mother, Mother! See here! What a lot of gold coins I've got. How many! How many!"

His mother, seeing the coins, and knowing very well that Vardiello would soon tell the world, told him to stand at the door until the man with milk and cheese came past, as she wanted to buy a penny's-worth of milk. So Vardiello, who was a great glutton, went quickly and seated himself at the door. And his mother showered down from the window above raisins and dried figs for more than half an hour. Vardiello picked them up as fast as he could, crying aloud, "Mother, Mother! Bring out some baskets; give me some bowls! Here, quick with the tubs and buckets! For if it continues to rain thus we shall be rich." And when he had eaten his fill, Vardiello went up to sleep.

It happened one day that two neighbors quarreled and went to court over a gold coin which they had found on the ground. Vardiello, passing by, said, "What jackasses you are to quarrel about money! For my part I don't value it a pin's head, for I've found a whole potful of coins."

When the judge heard this he opened wide his eyes and ears, and looked closely at Vardiello, asking him how, when, and where he had found the coins. Vardiello replied, "I found them in a palace, inside a silent man, when it rained raisins and dried figs." At this the judge stared with amazement. Instantly seeing how things were, he decreed that Vardiello should be sent to a madhouse for his own safety. Thus, even a stupid son

Vardiello and the Silent Man

can make mother rich, and the mother's wit saved her son's
neck, proving that—

> *A ship steered by a skillful hand*
> *Will seldom run into rock or sand.*

THE FLEA IN THE BOTTLE

ONCE upon a time, the King of High Hill, being bitten by a flea, caught him by a wonderful feat of dexterity. Seeing how handsome was the flea, the King had not the conscience to sentence him to death. So he put him into a bottle, and fed him every day himself. The little animal grew at such a rate that at the end of seven months it was necessary to shift his quarters, for he was grown bigger than a sheep. The King then had him killed and his skin dressed. Then he issued a proclamation that whoever could tell what this skin was should marry the Princess.

As soon as this decree was made known, the people flocked from all the ends of the world to try their luck. One said that it belonged to an ape, another to a lynx, a third to a crocodile. In short, some said one animal and some another. But they were all a hundred miles from the truth, and not one hit the nail on the head. At last, there came to this trial an ogre who was the most ugly giant in the world, the very sight of whom would make the boldest man tremble and quake with fear. But no sooner had he come and turned the skin round and smelled it than he instantly guessed the truth, saying, "This skin belongs to the King of Fleas."

Now the King saw that the ogre had hit the mark, and not to break his word, he ordered his daughter Porziella to be called. Porziella had a face like milk and roses, and was such a miracle of beauty that you would never tire of looking at her. And the King said to her, "My daughter, you know who I am. I cannot go back on my promise whether a man is a king or a beggar. I have given my word, and I must keep it though my heart should break. Who would ever have imagined that this prize would have fallen to an ogre! But it never does to judge hastily. Have patience and do not oppose your father, for my heart tells me that you will be happy, for rich treasures are often found inside a rough earthen jar."

When Porziella heard these sad words, her eyes grew dim, her face turned pale, her lips turned down, and her knees shook. At last, bursting into tears, she said to her father, "What crime have I committed that I should be punished thus? How have I ever behaved badly toward you that I should be given up to this monster? Is this, Father, the affection you bear to your own child? Is this the love you show to her whom you used to call the joy of your soul? Do you drive from your sight her who is the apple of your eye? O cruel father—It would have been better if I had died in my cradle than to live to see this evil day."

Porziella was beginning to say more when the King, in a furious rage, exclaimed, "Stay your anger! For appearances deceive. Is it for a girl to teach her father? How has a child hardly out of the nursery dared to oppose my will? Quick then, I say, take his hand and set off with him home this very instant, for I will not have your saucy face a minute longer in my sight."

Poor Porziella, seeing herself caught in the net, with the face of a person condemned to death, with the heart of one

The Flea in the Bottle

whose head is lying between the axe and the block, took the hand of the ogre, who dragged her off to the wood where the trees made a palace for the meadow to shelter it from the sun, and the brooks murmured knocking against the stones in the dark, while the wild beasts wandered where they liked and went safely through the thicket whither no man ever came unless he had lost his way. Upon this spot, as black as an unswept chimney, stood the ogre's house ornamented all round with the bones of the men whom he had devoured. Think for a moment of the horror felt by the poor girl.

But this was nothing compared with what was to come. For dinner, they had peas and dried beans. Then the ogre went out to hunt and returned home laden with the pieces of men whom he had killed, saying, "Now, Wife, you cannot complain that I don't take good care of you. Here is a fine store of eatables. Take and make merry and love me well, for the sky will fall before I will let you go hungry."

Poor Porziella could not endure this horrible sight and turned her face away. When the ogre saw this, he cried, "Ha! This is throwing sweetmeats before swine. Never mind. Only have patience till tomorrow morning, for I have been invited to a wild boar hunt and will bring you home a couple of boars, and we'll make a grand feast with our kinsfolk and celebrate the wedding." So saying, he went into the forest.

Now, as Porziella stood weeping at the window it chanced that an old woman passed by who, being famished with hunger, begged some food. "Ah, my good woman," said Porziella, "I am in the power of the ogre who brings me home nothing but pieces of the men he has killed. I am miserable, and yet I am the daughter of a king and have been brought up in luxury." And so saying, she began to cry like a little girl who sees her bread and butter taken away from her.

The old woman's heart was softened at this sight and she said to Porziella, "Be of good heart, my pretty girl, do not spoil your beauty with crying, for you have met with luck. Listen, now, I can help you. I have seven sons who are seven giants—Mase, Nardo, Cola, Micco, Petrullo, Ascaddeo, and Ceccone —who have more virtues than rosemary. Especially Mase, for every time he lays his ear to the ground he hears all that is passing within thirty miles. Nardo, every time he washes his hands, makes a great sea of soapsuds. Every time that Cola throws a bit of iron on the ground, he makes a field of sharp razors. Whenever Micco flings down a little stick, a tangled wood springs up. If Petrullo lets fall a drop of water, it makes a terrible river. When Ascaddeo wishes a strong tower to spring up, he has only to throw a stone. And Ceccone shoots so straight with the crossbow that he can hit a hen's eye a mile off. Now, with the help of my sons, who are all courteous and friendly, and who will all take compassion on your condition, I will free you from the claws of the ogre."

"No time better than now," replied Porziella, "for that evil husband of mine has gone out and will not return this evening, and we shall have time to slip off and run away."

"It cannot be this evening," replied the old woman, "for I live a long way off. But I promise you that tomorrow morning, I and my sons will all come together and help you out of your trouble."

So saying, the old woman departed, and Porziella went to

bed with a light heart and slept soundly all night. But as soon as the birds began to sing, "Long live the sun," lo and behold, there was the old woman with her seven children. Placing Porziella in their midst, they proceeded towards the city. They had not gone half a mile when Mase put his ear to the ground and cried, "Beware! Here's the fox. The ogre is come home. He has missed his wife and he is hastening after us."

No sooner did Nardo hear the warning than he washed his hands and made a sea of soapsuds. And when the ogre came and saw all the suds, he ran home and fetched a sack of bran, which he poured over the suds, treading it down with his feet until at last he got over this obstacle, though with great difficulty.

But Mase put his ear once more to the ground and exclaimed, "Look sharp, comrades, here he comes!" At that, Cola flung a piece of iron on the ground and instantly a field of razors sprang up. When the ogre saw that the path was blocked he ran home again and dressed himself in armor from head to foot. Then he returned and stalked through the razors.

Mase, again putting his ear to the ground, cried, "Up! Up! To arms! To arms! For the ogre is coming at such a rate that he is actually flying." But Micco was ready with his little stick. In an instant he caused a terrible wood to rise up, so thick that it was impenetrable. When the ogre came to this difficult passage he drew out his knife, which he always wore at his side, and began to cut down the poplars and oaks and pine trees and chestnut trees, right and left. With four or five strokes, he had the whole forest on the ground and was clear of it. Presently Mase, who kept his ears on the alert like a rabbit, again cried out, "We must be off, for the ogre is coming like the wind and here he is at our heels." As soon as Petrullo heard this, he took a drop of water from a little fountain, sprinkled it on the ground, and in the twinkling of an eye, a large river rose up on the spot. When the ogre saw this new obstacle, he stripped himself stark naked and swam across to the other side of the river carrying his clothes upon his head.

Mase, who now put his ear to every chink in the ground, heard the ogre coming and exclaimed, "Alas! I hear the clatter of the ogre's heels. We must be on our guard and ready to meet the storm or else we are done for." "Never fear," said Ascaddeo, "I will settle this ugly ragamuffin." So saying, he flung a pebble on the ground and instantly up rose a tower in which they all took refuge without delay, and barred the door. But when the ogre came up and saw that they had got into such a safe place he ran home, got a tall ladder, and carried it back on his shoulder to the tower.

Now Mase, who kept his ears hanging down, heard at a distance the approach of the ogre and cried, "We are now at the end of the Candle of Hope. Ceccone is our last resource, for the ogre is coming back in a terrible fury. Alas! How my heart pounds, for I foresee an evil day." "You coward," answered Ceccone. "Trust me and I will hit him with an arrow."

As Ceccone spoke the ogre came, planted his ladder against the tower, and began to climb up. Ceccone, taking aim, shot out one of his eyes and laid him full length on the ground, like a pear dropped from a tree. Then he went out and cut off the ogre's head with a big knife. They took the head with great joy to the King, who rejoiced at the recovery of his daughter, for he had repented a hundred times at having given her to an ogre. A few days later, Porziella was married to a handsome Prince, and the seven sons and their mother who had delivered her from such a wretched life were rewarded with great riches, proving once again that—

The child is sometimes wiser than the parent.

THE MERCHANT

THERE was once a very rich merchant named Antoniello, who had a son called Cienzo. One day Cienzo was throwing stones on the seashore with the son of the King of Naples, and by chance broke his companion's head. When he told his father, Antoniello flew into a rage with fear and berated his son. But Cienzo answered, "Sir, would it not have been worse if he had broken my head? It was he who provoked me. We are but boys, and there are two sides to the quarrel. After all it is a first offense, and the King is a man of reason. What great harm can he do me?"

But Antoniello would not listen to reason. He was sure the King would kill Cienzo for his crime. "Don't stand here at risk of your life," he said, "but march off this very instant, so that nobody may hear a word of what you have done. A bird in the bush is better than a bird in the cage. Here is money. Take one of the two enchanted horses I have in the stable, and the dog which is also enchanted. Tarry no longer. It is better to scamper off and use your own heels than to be hounded by another's. If you don't take your knapsack and be off, none of the saints can help you!"

Then begging his father's blessing, Cienzo mounted his horse and, tucking the enchanted dog under his arm, went on his way out of the city. Tearful and sighing he went his way

43

until nightfall, when he came to a dark wood, all silence and shadows. An old house stood there at the foot of a tower. Cienzo knocked at the door of the tower; but the master, being afraid of robbers, would not open the door. The poor boy was obliged to sleep in the ruined old house. He turned his horse out to graze in a meadow, and threw himself on some straw, with the dog by his side. But scarcely had he closed his eyes when he was awakened by the barking of the dog, and heard footsteps stirring in the house. Cienzo, who was a bold boy, seized his sword and began to swing it in the dark. Perceiving that he was only striking the wind, he stopped and lay down again to sleep. After a few minutes he felt himself tugged gently by the foot. He rolled over to reach again for his cutlass, and jumping up, exclaimed, "You are getting too troublesome! Stop this sport and let's have a bout if you have any pluck!"

He heard a shout of laughter and then a hollow voice saying, "Come down here and I will tell you who I am." Then Cienzo bravely answered, "I'll come." He groped about in the dark until he found a ladder which led into a cellar. Going down, he saw a lighted lamp, and three ghostlike figures who were wailing piteously, crying, "Alas, my beautiful treasure, I must lose thee!"

When Cienzo saw them he began to cry and lament along with them. After he had wept for some time, the moonlight having now broken through the dark sky showed clearly the three figures who were making the outcry. They said to Cienzo, "Take this treasure, which is destined for you only, but mind and take care of it." Then they vanished. Cienzo, seeing

The Merchant

the sunlight peeping through a hole in the wall, wished to climb up again, but he could not find the ladder. He set up such a cry that the master of the tower heard him and fetched a ladder. When he discovered the great treasure, he wished to give a part of it to Cienzo. But the boy refused. Taking his dog under his arm, he mounted his horse and set out again on his travels.

After a while he arrived at a wild and dreary forest, so dark that it made you shudder. There, upon the bank of a river, he found a fairy surrounded by a band of robbers. Cienzo seized his sword and killed them all. The fairy showered thanks upon him for this brave deed, and invited him to her palace that she might reward him. But Cienzo replied, "It is nothing at all; thank you kindly. Another time I will accept the favor, but now I must go in haste on important business."

So saying he took his leave. Traveling on a long way he came at last to the palace of a King, which was all hung with mourning, so that it made one's heart black just to look at it. When Cienzo asked the cause of the mourning the folks answered, "A dragon with seven heads has made his appearance in this country, the most terrible monster that ever was seen. He has a crest of a cock, the head of a cat, eyes of fire, the mouth of a bulldog, the wings of a bat, the claws of a bear, and the tail of a serpent. Now this dragon swallows a maiden every day. Today he has chosen Menechella, the daughter of the King. So there is great weeping and wailing in the royal palace, since the fairest creature in all the land is doomed to be devoured by this horrid beast."

As Cienzo heard this he saw Menechella pass by with the

mourning train, accompanied by the ladies of the court and all the women of the land, wringing their hands and tearing out their hair by handfuls, and bewailing the sad fate of the poor girl. Then the dragon came out of the cave. Cienzo laid hold of his sword and struck off one head. But the dragon went and rubbed his neck on a certain nearby plant, and suddenly the head joined itself on again. Seeing this, Cienzo exclaimed, "He who dares not, wins not." Gritting his teeth, he struck a furious blow that cut off all seven heads, which flew from the necks like peas popping from the pan. He cut out the tongues and put them in his pocket, flinging the heads a mile apart from the body, so they might never come together again. Then he sent Menechella home to her father, and went himself to rest in a nearby tavern.

When the King saw his daughter his delight was boundless. Having heard the story of how she had been freed, he ordered a proclamation to be instantly made: whosoever had killed the dragon should come and marry the Princess. Now a rascal of a country fellow, hearing this proclamation, collected the heads of the dragon and brought them to the King, saying, "I have saved Menechella. My hands have freed the land from destruction. Behold the dragon's heads, which are the proof of my valor. Therefore, remember, every promise is a debt." As soon as the King heard this, he lifted the crown from his own head and set it upon the fellow's head.

The news of this proclamation flew through the whole country, till at last it came to the ears of Cienzo, who said to himself, "I am a great blockhead! I had Fortune by the neck,

Vastolla and Peruonto Approaching the Ship
Page 24

Vardiello with the Cloth
Page 30

The Merchant

and I let her escape from my hand. Here's a man who offers to give me half of a treasure, and I care not; the fairy wishes to entertain me in her palace, and I care as little for it as an ass for music. And now that I am called to the crown, I stand here and let a rascally thief cheat me out of my reward!" So saying he took a pot of ink, seized a pen and, spreading out a sheet of paper, began to write:

TO THE MOST BEAUTIFUL JEWEL OF WOMEN, MENECHELLA——
Having saved thy life, I hear that another wears my feather in his cap and claims the reward of the service which I performed. You, who were present at the dragon's death, can tell the King the truth, and stop him from giving another this reward while I have had all the toil. For it will be the right outcome for thy fair royal grace and the deserved reward for this strong hero's fist. In conclusion, I kiss thy delicate little hands.
Sent from the Inn of the Flowerpot, Sunday

Having written this letter, and sealed it with wax, he placed it in the mouth of the enchanted dog, saying, "Run off as fast as you can and take this to the King's daughter. Give it to no one else, and place it in the hand of that silver-faced maiden herself."

Away ran the dog as if he were flying, and trotting up the stairs of the palace he found the King, who was still paying compliments to the country clown. When the King saw the dog with the letter in his mouth, he ordered it to be taken from him. But the dog would not give it up. Bounding up to

Menechella he placed the letter in her hand. Menechella rose from her seat, and, making a curtsey to the King, she gave him the letter to read. When the King had read it he ordered that the dog should be followed to see where he went, and that his master should be brought before him. Two courtiers immediately followed the dog, until they came to the tavern where they found Cienzo. Delivering the King's message, they conducted Cienzo to the palace, right into the presence of the King. The King demanded to know why he boasted of having killed the dragon, since the heads were brought by the man who was sitting at his side wearing a new crown. Cienzo answered, "That fellow deserves a cardboard hat rather than a crown, since he has had the impudence to tell you a bouncing lie. To prove to you that I have done the deed and not this rascal, order the heads to be produced. None of them can speak without a tongue, and I have brought these with me to convince you of the truth."

Saying this he pulled the tongues out of his pocket, while the country oaf was all confused, not knowing how it would all end. Menechella added, "This is the man! Ah, you dog of a countryman, a pretty trick you have played me!" When the King heard this, he took the crown from the head of that false loon and placed it on Cienzo's head. He was on the point of sending the impostor to jail, but Cienzo begged the King to have mercy on him and to match his wickedness with courtesy. Then Cienzo married Menechella, and the tables were spread for a royal banquet. In the morning they sent for Antoniello and all his family. Antoniello became a great

The Merchant

favorite of the King, and saw in the person of his son a man he could admire, proving the saying—

> *Even a ship that begins with a crooked course*
> *can reach a safe port.*

LITTLE GOAT-FACE

A PEASANT named Masaniello had twelve daughters, each one a half-head taller than the next; for every year their mother presented him with a little girl. The poor man, to support his family decently, went early every morning to work as a day laborer and dug hard the whole day long. With what his labor produced he just kept his little ones from dying of hunger.

He happened, one day, to be digging at the foot of a mountain that thrust its head above the clouds to see what they were doing up in the sky. He was working close to a cavern so deep and dark that the sun was afraid to enter it. Out of this cavern there came a green lizard as big as a crocodile; and the poor man was so terrified that he couldn't even move his legs to run away, expecting every moment the end of his days from one gulp of that ugly animal. But the lizard slowly approached him and said, "Be not afraid, my good man, for I am not come here harm you, but to do you good."

When Masaniello heard this, he fell on his knees and said, "Mistress Whatever-your-name-is, I am wholly in your power. Have pity on this poor trunk that has twelve branches to support."

"It is on this very account," said the lizard, "that I am here to serve you. Tomorrow morning bring me your youngest daughter, Renzolla, and I will rear her up like my own child, and love her as my life."

At this the poor father was more confounded than a thief when the stolen goods are found on his back. Hearing the lizard ask him for one of his daughters, and the tenderest of them, too, he concluded that she wanted the child as a tidbit to eat. He said to himself, "If I give her my daughter, I give her my soul. If I refuse her, she will swallow me up. If I consent, I am robbed of my heart; if I refuse, she takes my whole body. What shall I do? What course shall I take? Oh, what an ill day's work have I made of it! What misfortune has rained down upon me!"

While he was thinking, the lizard said, "Decide quickly and do what I tell you, or I will leave only your rags here. For so I will have it, and so it will be." Masaniello, hearing this demand, and having no one to help him, returned home feeling sad and low in his spirit. His wife, seeing him hanging his head like a sick bird and his shoulders like one that is wounded, said to him, "What has happened to you, Husband? Have you had a quarrel with someone? Is there a warrant for your arrest? Or is the donkey dead?"

"Nothing of that sort," said Masaniello, "but a giant lizard has put me into a fright, for she has threatened that if I do not bring her our youngest daughter, she will make me suffer. My head is spinning like a reel. I know not what turn to take. On one side, love constrains me. On the other, my family needs me. I love Renzolla dearly, and I love my own life dearly. But if I do not give the lizard this part of my heart, she will take my whole unfortunate body. So now, dear wife, advise me, or I am ruined!"

When his wife heard this, she said, "Who knows, Husband, but this may be a lizard that will make our fortune? Who knows but this lizard may put an end to all our miseries? How often, when we should have an eagle's sight to see good luck running to meet us, we have instead a veil over our eyes and a cramp in our hands when we should grasp it. So, go, take her away. For my heart tells me that some good fortune awaits the poor little thing!"

Her words comforted Masaniello. The next morning, as soon as the sun's rays whitewashed the sky which the shades of night had blackened, he took the little girl by the hand, and led her to the cave. The lizard came out, and taking the child gave the father a bag full of gold coins, saying, "Go now, be happy, for Renzolla has found both father and mother."

Masaniello, overjoyed, thanked the lizard and went home to his wife. There was money enough to help all the other daughters when they married, and the rest was gravy for the old folks to help them to swallow with relish the toils of life.

The lizard made a most beautiful palace for Renzolla, and brought her up in such state and magnificence as would have dazzled the eyes of any queen. She wanted for nothing. Her food was fit for a countess, her clothing for a princess. She had a hundred maidens to wait upon her. And with such good treatment she grew as sturdy as an oak tree. She was so spoiled that she took for granted all her good fortune.

It happened one day that the King was out hunting in those parts, and that night overtook him. As he stood looking

Little Goat-Face

round, not knowing where to lay his head, he saw a candle shining from the palace window. He sent one of his servants to ask the owner to give him shelter. When the servant came to the palace, the lizard appeared before him in the shape of a beautiful lady fairy. After hearing the request, she said that the king would be a thousand times welcome. The King, on hearing this reply, went to the palace and was received like royalty. A hundred pages went out to meet him, so that it looked like the funeral of a rich man. A hundred other pages brought the dishes to the table. A hundred others made a brave noise with musical instruments. But, above all, Renzolla served the King herself and handed him drink with such grace that he drank more love than wine.

Having been so royally entertained, the King he felt he could not live without Renzolla. So, calling the lady fairy, he asked her for Renzolla's hand. The fairy, who wished for nothing but Renzolla's good, freely consented, and gave her a dowry of seven bags of gold.

The King, overjoyed at this piece of good fortune, departed with Renzolla, who, ill-mannered and ungrateful for all the fairy had done for her, went off without uttering one single word of thanks. The lady fairy, beholding such ingratitude, cursed her, and wished that her face would become like a goat. Hardly had she uttered the words, than Renzolla's mouth stretched out, a long a beard grew from her chin, her jaws shrunk, her skin hardened, her cheeks grew hairy, and her golden braids turned into pointed horns.

When the poor King saw this he was thunderstruck, not knowing how such a great beauty could be so transformed.

With sighs and tears he exclaimed, "Where are the locks that bound me? Where are the eyes that entranced me? Must I be the husband of a goat? No, no, my heart shall not break for such a goat-face!" So saying, as soon as they reached his palace, he put Renzolla into the kitchen, along with a chambermaid, and gave each of them ten bundles of flax to spin, commanding them to have the thread ready at the end of a week.

The maid, in obedience to the King, set about carding the flax, combing and cleaning the fibers, then twirling and spinning without ceasing; so that on Saturday evening her thread was all done. But Renzolla, thinking she was still the same as in the fairy's house, not having looked at herself in the mirror, threw the flax out of the window, saying, "A pretty thing indeed for the King to give me such work! If he wants shirts let him buy them, and not think that he picked me up out of the gutter. I brought him home seven bags of gold, and I am his wife, not his servant. I think that he is a donkey to treat me this way!"

Nevertheless, when Saturday morning came, seeing that the maid had spun all her share of the flax, Renzolla was afraid. Away she went to the palace of the lady fairy and told her misfortune. Then the fairy embraced her with great affection, and gave her a bag full of spun thread to present to the King and show him what an industrious wife she was. Renzolla took the bag, and without saying one word of thanks, went back to the royal palace. Again the fairy was angry at the conduct of the graceless girl.

When the King had taken the thread, he gave two little dogs, one to Renzolla and one to the maid, telling them to feed and take care of them. The maid reared hers on bread crumbs and treated it like a child. But Renzolla grumbled, saying, "A pretty thing truly! Am I to comb and wait upon a dog?" And she flung the dog out of the window!

Some months later, the King asked for the dogs. Renzolla, losing heart, ran off again to the fairy. At the gate of the fairy's palace stood the old man who was the porter. "Who are you," he asked, "and whom do you want?" Renzolla, hearing herself addressed in this offhand way, replied, "Don't you know me, you old goat-beard?"

"Why do you miscall me?" said the porter. "This is the thief accusing the policeman. I, a goatbeard indeed! You are a goat-beard and then some. And you deserve the name, you impudent woman. Let me show you and you will see to what your ingratitude has brought you!"

So saying, he ran into his room, and taking a looking-glass, set it before Renzolla. When she saw her ugly, hairy reflection she almost died of fright. Her face was so altered that she did not know herself. The old man said to her, "You ought to remember, Renzolla, that you are a daughter of a peasant and that it was the fairy that raised you to be a queen. But you, rude, unmannerly, and thankless as you are, having little grati-tude for such high favors, have kept her waiting outside your heart, without showing her the slightest mark of affection. You have brought the trouble on yourself, and see what a face you have got by your ingratitude! For through the fairy's spell you have not only changed face, but your whole life. But if you will do as I advise, go and look for the fairy. Throw yourself at her feet, tear your beard, beat your breast, and ask

Renzolla threw herself at the feet of the fairy, who was moved by
her misfortune.

pardon for the ill treatment you have shown her. She is tender-hearted and she will be moved to pity by your misfortune.''

Renzolla, who was touched to the quick, followed the old man's advice. Then the fairy embraced and kissed her. Restoring her to her former appearance, she clad her in a robe heavy with gold; and placing her in a magnificent coach, accompanied by a crowd of servants, she brought her to the King. When the King beheld her, so beautiful and splendidly attired, he loved her as his own life. He blamed himself for all the misery he had made her endure, but also excused himself on account of that odious goat-face which had caused it. Thus Renzolla lived happily, loving her husband, honoring the fairy, and showing herself grateful to the old man, having learned to her cost that—

It is always good to show appreciation.

THE ENCHANTED DOE

THERE was once a certain King named Giannone, who greatly wished to have children. He prayed continually to the gods that they would grant his wish. To earn their favor he was so charitable to beggars and pilgrims that he shared with them all he possessed. But seeing, at last, that his generosity gained him nothing, and that there was no end to putting his hand into his pocket, he locked his door, and shot with a crossbow at all who came near.

Now it happened one day, that a long-bearded pilgrim was passing that way, and not knowing that the King had changed his attitude, or perhaps he did know it and wished to make him change his mind again, he went to Giannone and begged for shelter in his house. But, with a fierce look and terrible growl, the King said to him, "The kittens have their eyes open, and I am no longer a child." And when the old man asked the cause of this change, the King replied, "To fulfill my desire for children, I have lent to all who came, and have squandered all my treasure. Once the beard was gone, I stopped shaving and laid aside the razor."

"If that is all you ask," replied the pilgrim, "you may set your mind at ease, for I promise that your wish shall be fulfilled, or else I'll lose my ears."

"So be it," said the King, "If you can give me children, I

promise to give you one half of my kingdom." And the man answered, "Listen carefully. If you wish to hit the mark, you must get the heart of a sea dragon, and have it cooked and eaten by the Queen. And your wish will come true."

"That hardly seems possible," said the King. "But I lose nothing by trying. So I must, this very moment, get the dragon's heart."

The King sent a hundred fishermen out. They got ready all kinds of fishing tackle, drag nets, casting nets, bow nets, and fishing lines. They tacked and turned and cruised in all directions until at last they caught a sea dragon. Then they took out its heart and brought it to the King, who gave it to the Queen to cook and eat. And when she had eaten it, there was great rejoicing, for the King's desire was fulfilled and he became the father of two sons, so much alike that nobody but the Queen could tell which was which. And the boys grew up together with such love for one another that they could not be parted for a moment. Their attachment was so great that the Queen began to be jealous. The son destined to be heir to the throne, whose name was Fonzo, had more affection for his brother Canneloro than he did for her. And she did not know how to remove this thorn from her eyes.

Now one day Fonzo wished to go hunting with his brother, so he had a fire lighted in their chamber and began to melt lead to make bullets. While the lead was melting he went out to fetch a cup of water for himself and his brother. Meanwhile, the Queen came in, and finding no one there but Canneloro, she decided to put him out of the world. Stooping down, she flung the hot bullet-mold at his face, which hit him over the brow and made an ugly wound. She was about to repeat the blow when Fonzo came in. Pretending that she had only come in to see how he was, she gave him a kiss and went away.

Canneloro, pulling his hat down on his forehead, said nothing of his wound to Fonzo. He stood quietly though he was burning with pain. But as soon as they finished making the bullets, he told his brother that he must leave him. Fonzo, amazed at this resolution, asked him the reason. He replied, "Ask no more, my dear Fonzo, let it be that I must go away and part from you, who are my heart and soul and the breath of my body. Since it cannot be otherwise, farewell, and always remember me." Then after they embraced one another and shed many tears, Canneloro went to his own room. He armed himself from top to toe putting on a whole suit of armor and a sword and a dagger. Having taken a horse out of the stable, he was just putting his foot into the stirrup when Fonzo came out weeping. "Since you are resolved to abandon me," he said, "you should at least leave me some token of your love." Thereupon Canneloro struck his dagger into the ground, and instantly a fine fountain rose up. Then said he to his twin brother, "This is the best memorial I can leave you. By the flowing of this fountain you will follow the course of my life. If you see it run clear, know that my life is likewise clear and tranquil. If it is muddy, think that I am passing through troubles. And if it is dry, know that the water of my life is all used up and that I have paid the price!"

Then he drove his sword into the ground, and immediately a myrtle tree grew up. He said, "As long as this myrtle is green, know that I too am green as a green onion. If you see it wither, think that my fortunes are not the best in this world. And if it becomes dried up, you may mourn for your Canneloro."

So saying, after they embraced one another again, Canneloro set out on his travels. He journeyed on and on, with many adventures which it would be too long to tell. At length he arrived at the Kingdom of Clear Water, just at the time when they were holding a most splendid tournament, with the hand of the King's daughter being promised to the victor. Here Canneloro presented himself and performed so bravely that he overthrew all the knights who had come from all over the kingdom to make a name for themselves. Afterwards, he married the Princess Fenicia, and a great feast was made.

When Canneloro had lived there happily for some months, an unhappy fancy came into his head to go on a hunt. The King said to him, "Take care, my son-in-law, be wise and keep open your eyes, for in these woods is a most wicked ogre who changes his form every day. One time he appears like a wolf, another time like a lion, now like a stag, now like a donkey, first like one thing and now like another. By his wiley ways he tricks unlucky souls into a cave, where he devours them. So, my son, be careful, or you will leave your rags there."

Canneloro, who did not know what fear was, paid no heed to this advice. As soon as the sun had swept away the soot of the night he set out for the chase with a passel of hunting dogs running alongside his horse. On his way, he came to a wood where the thick awning of the leaves hid all the sunlight. The ogre, seeing him coming, turned himself into a handsome doe.

The Enchanted Doe

As soon as Canneloro saw her he began to give chase. The doe doubled and turned, and led him about hither and thither at such a rate, that at last she brought him into the very heart of the wood. There she raised such a tremendous snowstorm that it looked as if the sky would fall. Canneloro, finding himself in front of a cave, went in to seek shelter. Benumbed with the cold, he gathered some sticks which he found within, and pulling a flint from his pocket, he kindled a large fire. As he was standing by the fire to dry his clothes, the doe came to the mouth of the cave, and said, "Sir Knight, pray let me warm myself a little, for I am shivering with the cold."

Canneloro, who had a kindly disposition, said to her, "Draw near, and welcome."

"I would gladly," replied the doe, "but I am afraid you will kill me."

"Fear nothing," answered Canneloro, "trust to my word."

"If you wish me to enter," said the doe, "tie up those dogs, that they may not hurt me, and tie up your horse that he may not kick me."

So Canneloro tied up his dogs and hobbled his horse, and the doe said, "I am now half assured, but unless you bind fast your sword, I dare not come in." Then Canneloro, who wished to become friends with the doe, wrapped up his sword tightly in a blanket. As soon as the ogre saw Canneloro defenseless, he changed into his own form. Laying hold of him, he flung him into a pit at the bottom of the cave, and covered it over with a big rock. There he meant to keep Canneloro until he was ready to eat him up.

But back at home Fonzo, morning and evening visited the

myrtle and the fountain, to learn news of the fate of his brother. That evening, he found the myrtle withered, and the water of the fountain churned up with mud. Instantly he knew that his brother was in trouble. To help him, he mounted his horse without asking either his father or mother. Arming himself well and taking two enchanted dogs, he went rambling through the world. He roamed and rambled here, there, and everywhere until, at last, he came to Clear Water. All there were mourning for the supposed death of Canneloro. Scarcely had Fonzo come to the court, when everyone, thinking that he was Canneloro, hastened to tell Fenicia the good news. She ran leaping down the stairs, and embracing Fonzo cried, "My husband! My heart! Where have you been all this time?"

Fonzo immediately knew that Canneloro had been there and had left again. He listened as Fenicia lovingly scolded him for going hunting in the wood when he knew the ogre was about. And he instantly concluded that Canneloro must still be there.

The next morning, as soon as the sun touched the sky with light, he jumped out of bed. Neither the prayers of Fenicia, nor the commands of the King could keep him back. Mounting his horse, he went with the enchanted dogs to the wood, where the same thing befell him that had befallen Canneloro. Entering the cave, he saw his brother's sword wrapped up and the dogs and horse bound fast. Then the doe tried out the same ploy on him with which she had snared Canneloro, he instantly set the dogs upon her and they tore her to pieces. As he looked about for some trace of his brother, he heard his voice coming from down in the pit. Lifting up the stone, he drew out Canneloro, and all the others whom the ogre had buried alive to fatten. Then, embracing each other with great joy, the twin brothers went home. Fenicia, seeing them so much alike, did not know which one was her husband, until Canneloro took off his cap and she saw the mark of the old wound and recognized him. Fonzo stayed a month with them, enjoying their company. And then wished to return to his own country. Canneloro sent a letter with him, asking his mother to lay aside her jealousy and come and visit him and enjoy his great fortune, which she did. But from that time forward, he never again wanted to talk of dogs or hunting or does of any kind, remembering the saying—

He who learns the hard way learns best.

PARSLEY

THERE was, once upon a time, a woman named Pascadozzia, and one day, when she was standing at her window, which looked into the garden of an ogress, she saw such a fine bed of parsley that she almost fainted away with desire for some. So when the ogress left the house, Pascadozzia could not restrain herself any longer. Out she went into the garden and plucked a handful. The ogress came home and was going to cook her stew when she found that someone had been stealing the parsley. "I'll catch this long-fingered rogue," she said, "and make him repent it. I'll teach him that everyone should eat off his own platter and not meddle with other folks' cups."

Poor Pascadozzia went again and again down into the garden, until one morning the ogress met her, and in a furious rage exclaimed, "I have caught you at last, you thief! Tell me, do you pay the rent for the garden that you come in this impudent way and steal my plants? By my faith, I'll make you do penance without going to confession."

Poor Pascadozzia, in a terrible fright, began to make excuses. Neither gluttony nor hunger had tempted her to steal the parsley, she said. "I did it because I feared my child would be born with a crop of parsley on its face."

"Words are but wind," answered the ogress. "I am not

fooled by such prattle. You have closed the book on your life,
unless you promise to give me the child, girl or boy, whichever
it may be."

The poor woman, in order to escape the peril in which she
found herself, swore, by crossing her heart, to keep the promise. And so the ogress let her go free. But when the baby came
it was a little girl, so beautiful that she was a joy to look upon,
and Pascadozzia named her Parsley. The little girl grew from
day to day until, when she was seven years old, her mother sent
her to school. Every time she went along the street and met the
ogress the old woman said to her, "Tell your mother to remember her promise." She came home repeating this message
so often that the poor mother, no longer having patience to
listen to the refrain, said one day to Parsley, "If you meet the
old woman as usual, and she reminds you of the hateful promise, answer her, 'Take it.'"

Parsley had no idea what her mother meant, but when she
met the ogress again, and heard her repeat the same words, she
answered innocently as her mother had told her. Whereupon
the ogress seized her by her hair and carried her off to a dark
wood where sun never entered. Then she put the poor girl
into a tower which arose at her command. The tower had
neither gate nor ladder, but only a little window through
which the ogress climbed up and down by means of Parsley's
hair, which was very long, just as sailors climb up and down
the mast of a ship.

Now it happened one day, when the ogress had left the
tower, that Parsley leaned her head out of the little window
and let loose her tresses in the sun. The son of a Prince passing

Parsley

by saw that golden banner and in the midst of its gleaming waves, a face that enchanted all hearts. He fell desperately in love with such wonderful beauty. She told him all about her troubles, and implored him to rescue her. But a gossipy friend of the ogress, who was always poking her nose into every corner, overheard their secret. She told the ogress to be on the lookout, for Parsley had been seen talking with a certain youth, and she had her suspicions. The ogress thanked the gossip for the information. As for Parsley, she said, it was impossible for her to escape, as she herself had laid a spell upon her, so that unless she had in her hand three large nuts, called gallnuts, which were hidden in a rafter in the kitchen she could never get away.

While the ogress and the gossip were talking together, Parsley, who stood with her ears wide open, overheard all that they said. And when night had spread out her black garments, and the Prince had come at the appointed hour, she let fall her hair. He seized it with both hands, and cried, "Draw up." When he was drawn up through the small window the first thing she asked him to do was to climb onto the rafters and find the gallnuts. Then, on a rope ladder brought by the Prince, they both climbed down to the ground, took to their heels, and ran off toward the city. But the gossip, happening to see them come out, set up a loud shout and made such a noise that the ogress awoke. Seeing that Parsley had run away, she, too, descended by the same ladder, which was still fastened to the window, and set off after the couple. When they saw her coming at their heels galloping faster than a horse, they gave themselves up for lost. But then Parsley remembered the gallnuts, and quickly threw one on the ground. Lo, instantly a Corsican bulldog came bounding up—Oh, such a terrible beast! With open jaws and loud barking, he flew at the ogress as if to swallow her in one mouthful. But the old woman, who was more cunning and spiteful than ever, put her hand into her pocket, and pulling out a piece of bread gave it to the dog, which immediately quieted his fury and made him hang his tail.

Then she turned to run after the fugitives again. Parsley, seeing her approach, threw the second gallnut on the ground. And, lo, a fierce lion arose, who, lashing the earth with his tail, and shaking his mane and opening wide his jaws a yard apart, was just preparing to make a meal of the ogress, when she turned back quickly and stripped the skin off an ass which was grazing in the middle of a meadow; she ran at the lion, who thought she was a real jackass, was so frightened that he bounded and away as fast as he could.

The ogress having overcome this second obstacle turned again to pursue the poor lovers. Now, hearing the clatter of her heels, and seeing clouds of dust that rose up to the sky, they knew that she was coming again. But the old woman, who was every moment in dread lest the lion should pursue her, again, still wore the donkey's skin. When Parsley threw down the third gallnut there sprang up a wolf, who, without giving the ogress time to play any new trick, gobbled her up just as she was, in the shape of a jackass. So Parsley and the Prince, now freed from danger, went their way leisurely to the Prince's kingdom, where, after all these storms of fate, with his

Parsley

father's free consent, they were married. Thus, they experienced the truth that—

*After one hour in safe harbor, the sailor forgets all the fears
and dangers of a hundred years.*

THE THREE SISTERS

THERE was at one time a woman who had three daughters, two of whom were so unlucky that nothing ever succeeded with them. All their projects went wrong, all their hopes were turned to ashes. But the youngest, who was named Nella, was born to good luck, and at her birth all the gods conspired to bestow on her the best and choicest gifts. The Sky gave her the perfection of its light; Venus, matchless beauty of form; Love, the first dart of his power; Nature, the flower of manners. Nella never set about any work that did not come off nicely. She never took anything in hand that did not succeed. She never stood up to dance, that she did not sit down with applause. On this account she was envied by her jealous sisters, and yet not so much as she was loved by all others. As much as her sisters wished to bury her, so much more did other folks wish to lift her up in their arms.

Now there was in that country an enchanted Prince who was so attracted by Nella's beauty that he secretly married her. In order that they might enjoy one another's company without raising the suspicion of the mother, who was a wicked woman, the Prince made a crystal passage eight miles long which led from the royal palace directly into Nella's apartment. Then he gave her a magic powder saying, "Every time you wish to see me throw a little of this powder into the fire, and instantly I will come through the passage as quick as a bird, running along the crystal road to gaze upon your silvery face."

Not a night passed that the Prince did not go in and out, backwards and forwards, along the crystal passage, until at last the sisters, who were spying on Nella, found out the secret and laid a plan to put a stop to their happiness. They went along at once and broke the passage here and there. Now when the unhappy girl threw the powder into the fire to give the signal, to the Prince, who always came running in furious haste, cut himself against the broken crystal. Being unable to pass farther on he turned back all slashed and bleeding. Then he sent for all the doctors in the town. But as the crystal was enchanted the wounds were mortal, and no human remedy could heal them. When the King saw this, he despaired for his son's life. At once he sent out a proclamation that whoever would cure the wounds of the Prince—if a woman she should have the Prince for a husband—if a man he should have half his kingdom.

Now when Nella, who was pining away from the loss of the Prince, heard this she disguised herself by dirtying her face with ashes and running her sooty hands through her hair until it hung down like string and she looked like a poor ragamuffin. Then, unknown to her sisters, she left home to visit the Prince before his death. But by this time the sun's gilded ball, with which he plays in the fields of heaven, was running toward the west, and night overtook her in a dark wood, very near the house of an ogre. To avoid danger, she climbed up into a tree. Meanwhile the ogre and his wife were sitting at the dinner table with the windows open in order to enjoy the fresh air while they ate. As soon as they had emptied their cups and put out the lamps they began to chat of one thing and another, so that Nella, who was as near to them as the mouth is to the nose, heard every word they spoke.

Among other things, the ogress said to her husband, "My pretty Hairy Hide, tell me the news that is happening in the world?"

And he answered, "Trust me, everything's going topsy-turvy and all wrong."

"But what is it?" replied his wife.

"Why I could tell a thousand stories of all the confusion that is going on," replied the ogre, "for I have heard things enough to drive one mad, such as buffoons rewarded with gifts, rogues held in high esteem, cowards honored, robbers protected, and honest men neglected. But I will merely tell you what has befallen the King's son. He had made a crystal path along which he used to go to visit a pretty lass. But by some means or other, I know not how, all the road has been broken. And as he was going along the passage, he wounded himself in such a manner that before he will be able to stop the leak all the blood of his life will run out. The King has issued a proclamation making great promises to whoever cures his son. But it is all labor lost, and the best he can do is get ready for mourning and prepare the funeral."

When Nella heard the cause of the Prince's illness she sobbed and wept bitterly and said to herself, "Who is the wicked soul who has broken the passage and caused so much sorrow?" But as the ogress now began to speak Nella was as silent as a mouse and listened.

"Is it possible," said the ogress, "that the world is lost to this poor Prince, and that no remedy can be found for his malady?"

"Listen, Granny," replied the ogre, "the doctors cannot find remedies that surpass the bounds of nature. This is not a fever that will yield to medicine and diet, much less are these ordinary wounds which require ointment and bandage. The charm that was on the broken glass produces the same effect as onion juice on the tips of arrows, making the wound fatal. There is only one thing that could save his life, but don't ask me to tell it to you, for it is a secret."

"Do tell me, dear old Long Tusk," cried the ogress. "Tell me, if you would not see me die."

"Well then," said the ogre, "I will tell you provided you promise not to confide it to any living soul, for it would be the ruin of our house and the destruction of our lives."

"Fear nothing, my dear, sweet little husband," replied the ogress. "You shall sooner see pigs with horns and moles with eyes, than a single word shall pass my lips." So saying, she put one hand over her heart and swore to it.

"You must know then," said the ogre, "that there is nothing under the sun that can save the Prince from the snares of death, but our fat. If his wounds are anointed with this, his soul will stopped from leaving the dwelling of his body."

Nella, who overheard every word, waited for them to finish their chat. Then, getting down from the tree and taking heart, she knocked at the ogre's door crying, "Ah! My good masters, I pray you for charity, alms, some sign of compassion. Have a little pity on a poor, miserable, creature who is banished by fate far from her own country and deprived of all human aid, who has been overtaken by night in this wood and is dying of cold and hunger." And crying thus, she went on knocking and knocking at the door.

Upon hearing this deafening noise, the ogress was going to throw her half a loaf of bread and send her away. But the ogre, who was more greedy for flesh than the squirrel is for nuts, the bear for honey, the cat for fish, the sheep for salt, or the donkey for oats, said to his wife, "Let the poor creature come in, for if she sleeps in the fields, she may be eaten up by some wolf." In short, he talked so much that his wife finally opened the door for Nella. While the ogre pretended charity he was the whole time intending to make four mouthfuls of her. But first the ogre and his wife drank till they were fairly tipsy. When they fell asleep, Nella took a knife from a cupboard and made a hash of them. Then she put all their fat into a bottle and carried it straight to the court. Presenting herself before the King, she offered to cure the Prince. The King was overjoyed and led her to the chamber of his son. No sooner had Nella anointed him with the fat than the wound closed in a moment, just as if she had thrown water on a fire, and the Prince became sound and healthy.

When the King saw this, he said to his son, "This good woman deserves the reward I promised in the proclamation, and you will marry her." But the Prince replied, "It is hopeless. My heart is already disposed of, and another woman is already the mistress of it."

Nella, hearing this, replied, "You should forget her who has been the cause of all your misfortune."

"My misfortune has been brought on me by her sisters," replied the Prince, "and they shall suffer for it."

"Then do you really love her?" said Nella.

And the Prince replied, "More than my own life."

"Embrace me then," said Nella, "for I am the fire of your heart."

But the Prince, not recognizing Nella in her disguise, answered, "Keep away. Don't touch me." Whereupon Nella, perceiving that he did not know her, called for a basin of clean water and washed her face and hands and tied up her hair. As soon as the cloud of dirt was removed the sun shone forth. And the Prince, recognizing her at last, pressed her to his heart and acknowledged her for his wife. Then he had her sisters thrown into a dungeon, thus proving the truth of the old saying—

No evil ever goes without punishment.

The Princess as the Ogre's Bride
Page 37

The Prince Appearing to Nella
Page 74

PIPPO AND THE CLEVER CAT

THERE was one time in the beautiful city of Naples an old man who was as poor as poor could be. He was so wretched, so raggedy, and so frail, with not a penny in his pocket, that he went about naked as a flea. Being about to shake out the bags of life, he called to him his sons, Oratiello and Pippo, and said to them, "I am now called upon to pay the debt I owe to Nature. Believe me, I would be glad to quiet this house of misery, this den of woes, but that I must leave you behind—a pair of miserable fellows, as big as a church, without a stitch upon your backs, as clean as a barber's basin, as dry as a stone, without so much as a fly might carry upon its foot. Were you to run a hundred miles, not a penny would fall from your pockets. My ill fortune has brought me to such beggary that I lead the life of a dog. I have all my life gaped with hunger and gone to bed without a candle. Nevertheless, now that I am dying, I wish to leave you some token of my love. To you, Oratiello, who are my firstborn, I give the sieve that hangs against the wall, with which you can earn your bread. And to you, little fellow, take the cat and remember your daddy!" So saying, he began to whimper, and presently after said, "God be with you—for it is night!"

Oratiello had his father buried by charity, and then took the sieve and went here, there, and everywhere to gain a

79

Pippo and the Clever Cat

livelihood by using his sieve to separate the wheat from the chaff, helping the farmers and the bakers everywhere he went. The more he worked, the more he earned.

But Pippo, taking the cat, said, "What a pretty legacy my father has left me! I, who am not able to support myself, must now provide for two. What a miserable inheritance!"

The cat overheard this lamentation and said to him, "You needn't worry, for you have more luck than sense. I can make you rich if I set about it." When Pippo had heard this, he thanked Her Pussyship, stroked her three or four times on the back, and recommended himself warmly to her.

So the cat took compassion on poor Pippo. And every morning, when the sun, with the bait of light on his golden hook, fishes for the shades of night, she took herself down to the shore to catch a grey mullet, which she carried to the King. "My Lord Pippo," said the cat, "Your Majesty's most humble slave, sends you this fish with all reverence, and offers it as a small present for a great lord." Then the King, with the happy face that one usually shows to those who bring a gift, answered the cat, "Tell this lord, whom I do not know, that I thank him heartily."

Then, the cat would run to the marshes and the fields, and when the hunters brought down a blackbird or a lark, she caught it up and presented it to the King with the same message. She repeated this trick again and again, until one morning the King said to her, "I feel so obliged to this Lord Pippo, that I would like to meet him, so that I might return his kindness?"

And the cat replied, "My Lord Pippo only desires to give

80

Pippo and the Clever Cat

his life for Your Majesty; and tomorrow morning, without fail, as soon as the sun has set fire to the stubble of the fields, he will come and pay his respects to you."

When the morning came, the cat went to the King, and said to him, "Sire, my Lord Pippo begs to excuse himself for not coming, but last night some of his servants robbed him and ran off, and have not left him a single shirt to his back." When the King heard this, he instantly commanded his servants to take from his own wardrobe a quantity of clothes and linen, and sent them to Pippo. Two hours later, Pippo went to the palace, conducted by the cat, where he received a thousand compliments from the King, who made him sit beside himself, and gave him a banquet that would amaze you.

While they were eating, Pippo from time to time turned to the cat and said to her, "My pretty puss, pray take care that my old clothes don't slip through our fingers."

The cat answered, "Be quiet, be quiet. Don't be talking of these beggarly things."

The King asked to know the subject of their talk, and the cat answered that Pippo had taken a fancy to a small lemon, whereupon the King instantly sent out to the garden for a basketful. But Pippo soon returned to the same tune about the old coats and shirts, and the cat again told him to hold his tongue. When the King once more asked what was the matter, the cat had to make another excuse for Pippo's rudeness.

At last, when they had eaten and conversed for some time about one thing and another, Pippo took his leave; and the cat stayed with the King, describing the worth, the wisdom, and the judgment of Pippo. Above all, she told of his great wealth, which entitled him to marry even into the family of a crowned King. The King asked what might be his fortune, and the cat replied that no one could ever count all the valuables and fixtures and household furniture of this rich man, who did not even know how much he possessed. If the King wished to know the details, he had only to send messengers with the cat, and she would prove to him that there was no wealth in the world equal to his.

Then the King called some trusty persons, and commanded them to discover precisely the truth; so they followed in the footsteps of the cat. As soon as they had passed the frontier of the kingdom, from time to time the cat ran on ahead, pretending to provide refreshments for them on the road. Whenever she met a flock of sheep, a herd of cows, a troop of horses, or a drove of pigs, she would say to the herdsmen and keepers, "Ho! Have a care! A troop of robbers is coming to carry off everything in the country. If you wish to escape their fury, and protect your property, say that they all belong to the Lord Pippo, and not a hair will be touched."

She said the same thing at all the farmhouses, so that when the King's people came they heard the same tune piped. Everything they saw, they were told, belonged to the Lord Pippo. At last they were tired of asking, and returned to the King, telling about the seas and mountains of riches that belonged to Lord Pippo. The King, hearing this report, promised the cat a good drink if she could manage to bring about a marriage between his daughter and the rich Lord Pippo. The cat shuttled between them, and at last concluded the marriage agreement. So Pippo came, and the King gave him his daughter and a large portion of his kingdom.

At the end of a month of festivities, Pippo wished to take his bride away to his home. The King accompanied them as far as the frontier and then returned to his own palace. Pippo with his bride went on to Lombardy, where, by the cat's advice, Pippo purchased a large estate and became a baron.

Pippo, seeing himself now so rich, thanked the cat more than words can express, saying that he owed his life and his greatness to her good offices; and that the cleverness of a cat had done more for him than his own father. Therefore, said he, she might use him and his wealth as she pleased. And he gave her his word that when she died, which he prayed might not be for a hundred years, he would have her embalmed and put into a golden coffin, and set in his own chamber, that he might keep her memory always before his eyes.

The cat listened carefully to these lavish professions. Before three days she pretended to be dead, and stretched herself at full length in the garden. When Pippo's wife saw her, she cried out, "Oh, Husband, what a sad misfortune! The cat is dead!"

"Devil die with her!" said Pippo. "Better her than we!"

"What shall we do with her?" replied the wife.

"Take her by the leg," said he, "and fling her out of the window!"

Then the cat, who heard this fine reward when she least expected it, said, "Is this the return you make for my taking you from beggary? Are these the thanks I get for freeing you from rags? Is this my reward for having put good clothes on your back when you were a poor, starved, miserable ragamuffin? Go! A curse upon all I have done for you! A fine gold coffin you prepared for me! A fine funeral you were going to give me! Unhappy is he who does a good deed in hope of a return. The philosopher said it well: 'He who lies down a donkey, becomes a donkey himself.' He who does most, should expect least in return. Smooth words deceive both the fool and the wise man!"

So saying, she drew her cloak about her and went her way. Nothing that Pippo could do would soothe her. She would not return; but ran on and on without ever turning her head about, saying—

> *Heaven keep me from the rich grown poor,*
> *and from the beggar who becomes rich.*

GRANNONIA AND THE FOX

THERE was once upon a time a gardener's wife, who longed to have a son more than a person with a fever longs for water, or the innkeeper for the arrival of the mail coach.

It chanced one day that the gardener went to the mountain to get a bundle of wood, and when he came home and opened it he found a pretty little serpent lying among the twigs. At the sight of this, Sapatella (for that was the name of the gardener's wife) heaved a deep sigh, and said, "Alas! Even the serpents have their little serpents; but I brought ill luck with me into this world." At these words, the little serpent spoke, and said, "Well, then, since you cannot have children, take me for a child, and you will make a good bargain, for I shall love you better than my mother."

Sapatella, hearing a serpent speak, nearly fainted. But, plucking up her courage, she said, "For nothing more than the affection which you offer, I am content to take you, and treat you as if you were really my own child."

So saying, she gave him a hole in a corner of the house for a cradle, and fed him a share of her own food with the greatest goodwill in the world.

The serpent increased in size from day to day; and when he had grown pretty big, he said to Cola Matteo, the gardener, whom he looked on as his father, "Papa, I want to get married."

"I approve, with all my heart," said Cola Matteo. "We must look out for another serpent like yourself, and try to make up a match between you."

"What serpent are you talking of?" said the little serpent.

"I suppose, we are all the same among the vipers and adders! It is easy to see you are nothing but a country bumpkin. I want the King's daughter. Go this very instant and ask the King for her, and tell him it is a serpent who demands her."

Cola Matteo, who was a plain, straightforward kind of man, went innocently to the King and delivered his message, saying, "Know then that a serpent wants your daughter for his wife, and I am come to try to see if we can make a match between a serpent and a dove!" The King, who saw at a glance that Cola Matteo was a blockhead, to get rid of him, said, "Go and tell the serpent that I will give him my daughter if he turns all the fruit of this orchard into gold." And so saying, he burst out laughing, and dismissed him.

When Cola Matteo went home and delivered the answer to the serpent, he replied, "Go tomorrow morning and gather up all the fruit pits you can find in the city, and plant them in the orchard, and you will see pearls appear on rushes!"

Cola Matteo, who was no magician, neither knew how to comply nor refuse. So next morning, as soon as the sun with his golden broom had swept away the dirt of the night from the fields he took a basket on his arm and went from street to street, picking up all the pits that he could find—peaches, plums, nectarines, apricots, and cherries. He then went into the orchard of the palace and planted them, as the serpent had instructed. In an instant the trees shot up, and stems and branches, leaves, flowers, and fruit were all of glittering gold. The King was in an ecstasy at the sight and cried aloud with joy.

But when the serpent sent Cola Matteo back to the King, to demand his promise, the King said, "Wait, I must first have something else if he would have my daughter. He must make all the walls and the ground of the orchard turn into precious stones."

When the gardener told this to the serpent, he said, "Go tomorrow morning and gather up all the bits of broken crockery you can find, and throw them on the walks and on the walls around the orchard. We will not let this small difficulty stand in our way."

As soon as it grew dark, Cola Matteo put a basket over his arm, and went about collecting bits of broken jars, pieces of plates and dishes, handles of jugs, and spouts of pitchers. He picked up all the spoiled, broken, cracked lamps and all the fragments of pottery he could find and cast them all about the golden orchard. When he had done all that the serpent had told him, the walls around and the earth beneath the golden trees were mantled with emeralds and pearls, and coated with rubbies and sapphires until their luster dazzled your eyes. The King was so struck by the sight, he knew not what had befallen him. But when the serpent once again demanded that he keep his promise, the King answered, "Oh, all of this is nothing, if the palace isn't turned into solid gold."

When Cola Matteo told the serpent about the King's new

fancy, the serpent said, "Go and get a bundle of herbs and rub the bottom of the palace walls with them. We shall see if we cannot satisfy this new whim!"

Away went Cola that very moment, and made a great broom of cabbage leaves, radishes, onions, parsley, turnip tops, and carrots. And when he had rubbed the lower part of the palace with it, instantly you could see it shining like a golden ball. And when old Cola came again to demand the hand of the Princess, the King, seeing no other recourse, finally called his daughter. "My dear Grannonia," the king said, "I have tried to get rid of a suitor who asked to marry you, by making such conditions as seemed impossible for him to meet. But I am beaten, and must consent, I pray you, as you are a dutiful daughter, to allow me to keep my word, and to be content with what Fate wills and what I must obliged to do."

"Do as you please, Father," said Grannonia. "I shall not oppose a single jot of your will!" The King, hearing this, told Cola Matteo have the serpent come.

The serpent set out for the palace, lying on top of a gold wagon, drawn by four golden elephants. But wherever he came the people fled in terror, seeing such a large and frightful serpent being carried through the city. When he arrived at the palace, the royal relatives and courtiers all trembled like rushes and ran away; and even the very kitchen servants did not dare to stay in the place. The King and Queen, also shivering with fear, crept into their chamber. Only Grannonia stood her ground. Although her father and mother cried, "Fly, fly, Grannonia, save yourself," she would not stir from the spot. "Why should I fly from the husband you have given me?" she asked. And when the serpent came into the room, he wrapped his tail around Grannonia's waist, and gave her such a shower of kisses that the King turned as pale as Death. Then the serpent carried her into another room and locked the door. Shaking off his skin and letting it fall to the floor, he became a most beautiful youth, with a head covered with golden ringlets and with eyes that would enchant you!

When the King saw the serpent take his daughter into the room and shut the door after him, he said to his wife, "Heaven have mercy on our child! That evil serpent will swallow her down like the yolk of an egg." Then he put his eye to the keyhole to see what had become of her. When he saw the handsome youth, and the skin of the serpent lying on the ground, he kicked in the door, rushed in, with his wife and flung the skin into the fire and burned it.

When the youth saw this, he cried, "Ah, fool, what have you done!" Instantly he was turned into a dove and flew blindly at the window pane, striking his head and cutting himself sorely.

Grannonia was at the same moment happy and unhappy, joyful and miserable, rich and poor. She tore her hair and bewailed her fate, reproaching her father and mother; but they excused themselves, declaring that they had not meant to do harm. But she went on weeping and wailing until it grew dark. When they were all in bed, Grannonia disguised herself in the shawl of a peasant, and went out by the back door, to search everywhere for the husband she had lost.

She went out of the city, guided by the light of the moon; and on her way she met a fox, who asked her if she wished for company. "Of all things, my friend," replied Grannonia, "I should be delighted, for I am not familiar with the countryside." So they traveled along together till they came to a wood, where the trees were making arches for the shadows to lie under. And as they were now tired and wished to rest, they sheltered under the leaves where a fountain was playing tricks with the grass, throwing water on it by the dishful. They stretched themselves on a mattress of tender soft grass, and went to sleep.

They did not awaken till the Sun, with his usual fire, gave the signal that it was time to resume their travels. But even after they awoke, they lingered for some time listening to the songs of the birds, in which Grannonia took great delight. The fox said to her, "You would enjoy it twice as much if, like me, you understood what they were saying. At these words Grannonia begged the fox to tell her what he had heard the birds saying. After letting her plead for a long time, to raise her curiosity further, he told her that the birds were talking to each other about a King's son, who was as beautiful as a jay. Because he had offended a wicked ogress, she had laid him under a spell to spend seven years in the form of a serpent. When the seven years had nearly passed, he fell in love with the daughter of another King. Being one day alone in a room with the maiden, he had cast his skin on the ground; but her father and mother had rushed in and burned it. Then, when the Prince was trying to fly away in the shape of a dove, he broke a pane in the window, and hurt his head so severely that he was dying.

Grannonia, hearing her own story told back to her, asked if there was any cure for this injury. The fox replied that only if his wounds could be bathed with the blood of those very birds that were telling the story might the Prince be saved. When Grannonia heard this, she fell down on her knees, entreating the fox to catch those birds for her, that she might get their blood. She added that they would share the gain. Said the fox, "Let us wait till night, and when the birds are gone to bed, trust me to climb the tree and capture them, one after the other."

So they waited till day was gone, and Earth had spread out the night like a great black board. As soon as the fox saw all the birds fast asleep on the branches, he stole up quite softly, and one after another throttled all the larks, blackbirds, woodpeckers, thrushes, jays, little owls, goldfinches, bullfinches, and redbreasts that were on the trees. And when he had killed them all they put the blood in a little bottle, which the fox carried with him.

Grannonia was so overjoyed that her feet hardly touched the ground. But the fox said to her, "What fine joy in a dream is this, my daughter! You can do nothing, unless you mix my blood with that of the birds." And so saying he set off to run away.

Grannonia, who saw all her hopes fleeing away with him, resorted to a clever ruse. "Dear fox," she said, "you would have good reason to worry if I did not owe you so much, and if there were no other foxes in the world. But you know I am in your debt, and there are many more foxes on these plains. Trust me. Like the cow that kicks over the pail which she has just filled with milk, you have done the chief part, and now you fail at the last. Wait for me! And come with me to the city of this King."

The fox never dreamed that he could be out-foxed by any-one. So he agreed to travel on with her. But they had hardly gone fifty paces, when she lifted up the stick she carried and gave him such a neat rap that he fell over dead. Then she put his blood into the little bottle, and setting off again she went straightway to the royal palace, and sent word that she was come to cure the Prince.

Then the King ordered her to be brought before him, he was astonished to see a young woman undertake a cure which the best doctors in his kingdom had failed to do. However, it could do no harm to try. He said he wished immediately to see the experiment made.

But Grannonia answered, "If I succeed, you must promise to give him to me for a husband."

The King, who believed that his son would die, answered her, "If you give him to me safe and sound, I will give him to you sound and safe. For it is easy to give a husband to her that gives me a son."

So they went to the chamber of the Prince where he was lying in the dark, his life ebbing away. As soon as Grannonia anointed him with the blood, he was as good as new. When she saw the Prince stout and hearty again, Grannonia bade the King keep his word. Turning to his son, the king said, "My son, a moment ago you were all but dead, and now I see you alive, and can hardly believe it. Therefore, as I have promised this maiden that if she cured you she should have you for a husband, by all the love you bear me, help me keep my promise, since gratitude obliges me to pay this debt.''

When the Prince heard these words, he said, "Sir, I wish that I was free to prove to you the love I bear you. But I have already pledged my faith to another woman, and I know you would not want me to break my word, nor would this maiden wish me to wrong the woman I love. Nor can I change the way I feel!''

Grannonia felt a secret pleasure to learn she was still alive in the memory of the Prince. She blushed and said, "If I could induce this maiden to give up her claim to you, would you agree to marry me?''

"Never,'' replied the Prince, "will I banish from my heart the fair image of her whom I love. I shall ever remain of the same mind and will. And I would sooner see myself in danger of losing my place at the table of life than play so mean a trick!''

Grannonia could no longer hide her face. In the darkened chamber the Prince had not known her. But now, as she removed the peasant's shawl from around her head, he suddenly recognized her, and embraced her with a joy that would amaze you, telling his father all he had done and suffered for her. Then they invited her parents, the King and Queen of Long Field to celebrate the wedding with wonderful festivity, making great sport of that great ninny of a fox, and concluding at last that—

> *Pain is but a seasoning that proves*
> *the joys of constant love.*

THE SHE-BEAR

ONCE upon a time there lived a King of Rough Rock, who had a beautiful wife, but as she grew older she fell from the horse of health and broke her life. Before the candle of life went out she called her husband and said to him, "I know you have always loved me tenderly; show me, therefore, at the close of my days the depth of your love by promising me never to marry again, unless you find a woman as beautiful as I have been. Otherwise I leave you my curse, and shall bear you hatred even in the other world."

Hearing her last wish, the King, who loved his wife beyond measure, burst into tears, and for some time could not answer a single word. At last, when he had done weeping, he said to her, "Before I take another wife may the gout cripple me; may I have my head cut off like a mackerel! My dearest love, drive such a thought from your mind. Do not believe that I could love any other woman. You were the first new coat of my love, and you shall carry away with you the last rags of my affection."

As he said these words the poor Queen, who was at the point of death, turned up her eyes, stretched out her feet, and died. When the King saw her life thus running out he unstopped his tears, and made such a howling and beating and outcry that all the Court came running up, calling out the name of the dear Queen, and upbraiding Fortune for taking her from the King. Plucking out his beard, the King cursed the stars that had sent him such a misfortune.

But bearing in mind the maxim, "Pain in one's elbow and pain for one's wife are both hard to bear, but are soon over," before the night was over he began to count upon his fingers and reflect to himself. "Here is my wife dead," he thought, "and I am left a wretched widower, with no hope of seeing anyone but this poor daughter whom she has left me. I must try to find some way to have a son and heir. But where shall I look? Where shall I find a woman equal in beauty to my wife? Everyone is a witch in comparison with her. Where, then, shall I find another if Nature made Nardella (may she be in Heaven), and then broke the mold? Alas, in what a perplexity has the promise I made her left me! But what am I saying? I am running away before I have seen the wolf. Let me open my eyes and ears and look about. Is it possible that the world should be lost to me? Is there such a dearth of women, or is the race extinct? There may yet be some other as beautiful."

So saying, he issued a proclamation and commanded that all the beautiful women in the world should come to Rough Rock, for he would take the most beautiful to be his wife and endow her with a kingdom. Now, when this news was spread abroad, there was not a woman in the universe who did not come to try her luck—not a witch, however ugly, who stayed behind; for when it is a question of beauty, no scullion-maid will acknowledge herself surpassed. Every one prides herself on being the handsomest. And if the looking-glass tells her the truth she blames the glass for being untrue, and the quicksilver for being laid on badly.

When the town was filled with women the King had them all drawn up in a line, and he walked up and down the line from one end to the other. As he examined and measured each from head to foot none satisfied him. One appeared wrinkled, another long-nosed, another wide-mouthed, another thick-lipped, another tall as a may-pole, another short as a mushroom, another too stout, another too slender. This one did not please him on account of her dark eyes, that one was not to his fancy on account of her gait; this one appeared cold and icy, that one frivolous and giddy, the last with her light hair looked like a sheaf of wheat. One after the other, he sent them all away. And, seeing that so many fair faces were all show and no wool, he turned his thoughts to his own daughter, saying, "Why do I go seeking the impossible when my daughter Preziosa is formed in the same mold of beauty as her mother? Why go looking all around the world when I have this fair face right here in my house. She shall marry whom I choose, and so I shall have an heir."

When Preziosa heard this she locked herself in her room and bewailed her bad luck. While she was lamenting, an old woman came to her window, and hearing the cause of her grief, said to her, "Cheer up, my child, do not despair. There is a remedy for every problem. Now listen: if your father speaks to you thus once again put this bit of wood into your mouth, and instantly you will be changed into a she-bear. Then off with you! In his fright he will let you depart. Then run straight to the wood, where Heaven has kept good fortune in store for you since the day you were born. Whenever you wish to change back into a woman, only take the piece of wood out of your mouth and you will return to your true form."

Preziosa embraced the old woman, and, filling her apron with oats, and ham and bacon, sent her away.

As soon as the sun began to set, the King ordered the musicians to come, and, inviting all his lords and vassals, he held a great feast. And after dancing for five or six hours, they all sat down at the table, and ate and drank their fill. Then the King asked his courtiers to whom he should give Preziosa, as she was the picture of his dead wife. The instant Preziosa heard this, she slipped the bit of wood into her mouth, and turned into a terrible she-bear, at the sight of which all present were frightened out of their wits, and ran off as fast as they could scamper.

Meanwhile, Preziosa ran out, and made her way to a wood, where the shades were deciding what tricks to play on the sun at the close of day. There she stayed, in the pleasant company of the other animals, until the son of the King of Running Water came to hunt in that part of the country. At the sight of the bear, he nearly died on the spot. But when he saw the beast come gently up to him, wagging her tail like a little dog and rubbing her side against him, he took courage, and patted her. "Good bear, good bear!" he said. "There, there! Poor beast, poor beast!" Then he led her home and ordered his servants to take good care of her. He had her put into a garden close to the royal palace, that he might see her from the window whenever he wished.

One day, when all the other people of the house were out,

and the Prince was left alone, he went to the window to look out at the bear. There he beheld Preziosa, who had taken the piece of wood out of her mouth, combing her golden tresses. At the sight of this beauty, he nearly lost his senses and, tumbling down the stairs, he ran out into the garden. But Preziosa saw him coming, popped the piece of wood into her mouth, and was instantly changed into a bear again.

When the Prince came out and looked about for Preziosa, whom he had seen from the window above, a deep sadness came over him. In four days he fell sick, crying continually, "My bear, my bear!"

His mother, hearing him wailing, imagined that the bear had done him some harm. She gave orders for the bear to be killed. But the servants, who loved the tame bear, took pity on her. Instead of killing her, they led her into the wood, and told the Queen that they had put an end to her.

When the Prince heard this, he jumped out of bed, and went to make mincemeat of the servants. But when they told him the truth, he jumped on horseback, half-dead as he was, and rambled about looking everywhere, until at last he found the bear. Then he took her home again, and putting her into a chamber, said to her, "O lovely morsel for a King, who art shut up in this skin! Do you wish to see me pine and pant, and die by inches? I am wasting away, without hope, tormented by thy beauty. I am shrunk two-thirds in size, like wine boiled down, and am nothing but skin and bone. So lift up the curtain of this hairy hide, and let me gaze upon the spectacle of thy beauty! Raise, O raise the leaves off this basket, and let me see the fine fruit beneath! Part that curtain, and let my eyes behold the sumptuous wonders! Who has locked up so rich a treasure in a leathery chest? Let me behold this display of graces, and in return take all my love; for nothing else can cure my troubles."

But when he saw that all his words were useless, he took to his bed, and had such a desperate fit that the doctors didn't know how to help him. His mother sat down by his bedside, and said to him, "My son, whence comes all this grief? You are young, you are loved, you are great, you are rich—what is it you want, my son? Speak; a bashful beggar carries an empty bag. If you want a wife, only choose, and I will bring the match about. Take whatever you want, and I will pay. Do you not see that your illness is an illness to me? Your pulse beats with fever in your veins, and my heart beats with illness in my brain. So be cheerful now, and cheer up my heart, and do not let the whole kingdom be thrown into mourning, and your mother forlorn and heartbroken."

When the Prince heard these words, he said, "Nothing can console me but the sight of the bear. Therefore, if you wish to see me well again, let her be brought into this chamber. I will have no one else to attend me, and make my bed, and cook for me, but the bear herself. You may be sure that this pleasure will make me well in a minute."

Thereupon his mother, although she thought it was ridiculous for the bear to act as cook and chambermaid, and feared that her son was not in his right mind, had the bear fetched. And when the bear came up to the Prince's bed, she raised her paw and felt the Prince's forehead, which made the Queen laugh out loud, for she thought the bear would scratch his nose.

Then the Prince said, "My dear bear, will you not cook for me, and give me my food, and wait upon me?" And the bear nodded her head, to show that she accepted the job. The Prince's mother had some chickens brought, and a fire lighted on the hearth in the same chamber, and some water set to boil. The bear, taking up a chicken, scalded and plucked it, then stuck half of it on the spit to roast. With the other half she made such a delicious chicken hash that the Prince, who wouldn't even eat candy, ate it all up and licked his fingers afterward. When he had done eating, the bear handed him drink with such grace that the Queen was ready to kiss her.

Thereupon the Prince arose, and the bear quickly made the bed. And running into the garden, she gathered a clothful of roses and lemon blossoms and scattered them over the bed clothes, so that the Queen said the bear was worth her weight in gold, and that her son had good reason to be fond of her.

But when the Prince saw the bear's pretty behavior, it only added fuel to the fire. Before he had wasted away by ounces, now he melted away by pounds. He said to the Queen, "My lady mother, if I do not give this bear a kiss, the breath will leave my body."

The Queen, seeing him fainting away, said to the bear, "Kiss him, kiss him, my beautiful beast! Let my poor son not die of longing."

Then the bear went up to the Prince and, placing her paws on his cheeks, kissed him again and again. Meanwhile (I know not how), the piece of wood slipped out of her mouth, and

The She-Bear

Preziosa remained in the arms of the Prince, the most beautiful woman in the world. Pressing her to his heart, he said, "I have caught you, my little rogue! You shall never escape from me again."

At his words Preziosa said to him, "I am indeed in your hands—only guard me safely, and marry me when you will."

Then the Queen asked who the beautiful maiden was, and what had brought her to her rough disguise. Preziosa told the whole story of her misfortunes. The Queen, praising her as a good and virtuous woman, told the Prince that she was content that Preziosa should be his wife. The Prince, who wanted nothing more in the world, pledged her his faith. And the Queen gave them her blessing and this happy marriage was celebrated with great feasting and dancing and Preziosa knew that the old saying was true—

One who behaves well may always expect good fortune.

FILADORO AND THE DOVE

ABOUT eight miles from Naples there was once a deep wood where fig trees and poplars grew. In this wood stood a half-ruined cottage; and inside the cottage lived a toothless old woman with a hundred wrinkles in her face, and all her silver upon her head, so that she went from one thatched cottage to another, begging pennies to keep life in her. But as folks nowadays would rather give a purse full of gold coins to a clever rogue than a cent to a poor needy woman or man, she had to toil a whole day just to get a dish of red beans, which as you know were very plentiful in those days, as they are even today.

Now, one day, the poor old woman, after having washed the beans, put them in a pot, placed it outside the window to soak, and went into the wood to gather sticks for the fire. While she was away, Nardo Aniello, the King's son, passed by the cottage on his way to go hunting. Seeing the pot sitting on the window sill, he made a bet with his friends to see who could hit the pot with a stone. Then they began to throw rocks at the innocent pot. In three or four tries, the Prince hit it and broke the pot into pieces. Laughing, Nardo Aniello collected his bet from his friends, and they went on their way.

When the old woman returned home and saw the sad disaster, she began to cry. "Oh, the villainous rascal who has

103

broken my only pot and thrown my beans in the dirt! Even if
he has no feeling for my misery, he should at least worry about
his own best interests. For I pray to Heaven, on my bare knees
and from the bottom of my soul, that he will fall in love with
the daughter of an ogress, who will torment him in every way.
May his mother-in-law lay on him such a curse that he will
wish he were dead. May she order him about with a club in
her hand and feed him only a bit of bread with a tiny fork.
May he be so spellbound that he will be unable to escape.
Then he will wish he had my poor beans to eat, instead of
spilling them all over the ground."

The old woman's cries took wing and flew up to Heaven.
Scarcely had two hours passed when the Prince lost his way in
the woods, and became separated from his friends. He came
upon a beautiful maiden who was sitting on the cool green
grass, reviewing a long parade of snails, with handsome bright
shells; and she was singing to them, saying:

> *"Snail, snail, put out your horn,*
> *Your mother is calling you home,*
> *To see your brother who has just been born."*

When Nardo Aniello saw this beautiful vision he fell under
her spell and his heart was aflame with desire. Now, the
maiden, who was called Filadoro, was an ordinary girl. The
handsome and clever young Prince immediately captured her
heart, so that they stood looking at one another for a long
time, unable to utter a single word. The Prince, at last finding
his voice, said, "From what meadow has this flower sprung?

104

Filadoro and the Dove

From what deep mine has this jewel come to light? O happy woods, wherein this queenly beauty lives."

"My lord," answered Filadoro, "all the praise that you bestow on me truly belongs to you. Whatever I am, handsome or ugly, fat or thin, I am at your command, for you have captured my heart and from this moment on I give myself to you forever."

Hearing her words, the Prince seized her hands in his own and Filadoro blushed until her cheeks grew red as scarlet. Just at this moment Filadoro's mother suddenly appeared; she was such an ugly ogress that she was the very model of horrors. Her hair was like a broom; her forehead like a rough stone; her eyes were black coals full of evil; her mouth had tusks like a wild boar. In short, from head to foot, she was ugly beyond imagination. Now she seized Nardo Aniello by the nape of his neck, saying, "What now, you thief! You rascal!"

"Get back, old hag," replied the Prince. He was about to draw his sword, when all at once he stood frozen in his tracks like a sheep that has seen a wolf and can neither run nor cry for help. Holding him around the neck, the ogress led him like a donkey to her house. And when they arrived she said to him, "Unless you wish to die like a dog, you will have to work like a dog. Your first job today is to plow this whole acre of land and plant it in perfect rows. If the work is not finished when I come back tonight, I will eat you up." Then, telling her daughter to take care of the house, she went out into the woods to a meeting of the other ogresses.

Nardo Aniello began to weep, cursing his fate. But Filadoro comforted him, telling him to be of good heart, for she would risk her life to help him. She loved him so dearly, she said, how could he be sorry they had met?

The Prince replied: "I am not sorry to have traded the royal palace for this hut; splendid banquets for a crust of bread; my golden staff for a shovel. I consider myself lucky just to be with you. But what pains me to the heart is that I have to dig till my hands are covered with calluses; and, what is worse, I have to do more work than two oxen could do, all in one day. If I do not finish the task this evening, your mother will eat me up."

So saying he heaved a great sigh and shed many tears. But Filadoro, drying his eyes, said to him, "My mother will not touch a hair of your head. Trust me and do not be afraid. I possess magical powers. Be of good heart and by tonight the land will be dug and planted without your lifting a hand."

When Nardo Aniello heard this, he answered, "If you have magic powers, as you say, O beauty, why do we not fly away from here? You shall live like a queen in my father's house."

Filadoro replied, "For now, the stars prevent it; but the trouble will soon pass and we shall be happy."

The Prince talked away the afternoon with the beautiful Filadoro. As evening fell the ogress came back, calling to her daughter from outside the high tower of the house. "Filadoro, let down your hair," for as the house had no staircase, she always climbed up by her daughter's tresses. As soon as Filadoro heard her mother's voice she untied her hair and let down her tresses, making a golden ladder. The old woman climbed up quickly, and looked out into the field. When she saw it all plowed and planted she was beside herself with

Filadoro and the Dove

amazement. It seemed impossible that such a delicate lad could have accomplished such a hard task.

But, the next morning, hardly had the sun come out than the ogress went out again, telling Nardo Aniello to split six stacks of wood which were in the cellar, and to make sure each log was cut into four equal pieces before she returned that evening, or else she would cut him up like bacon and fry him for supper.

On hearing her command, the poor Prince nearly died of terror. Filadoro, seeing him pale as ashes, said, "What a coward you are to be frightened at such a trifle."

"You think it is a trifle to split six stacks of wood, with every log cut into four equal pieces, before nightfall?"

"Fear not," answered Filadoro, "for without you lifting a hand the wood shall all be split in time. Meanwhile, cheer up, if you love me, and stop your worrying."

Now when the Sun had shut up shop for the day the horrid old woman returned. Calling for Filadoro to let down the ladder of her hair as usual, she climbed up. When she saw the wood already split and neatly piled up, each log perfectly divided into four equal pieces, she grew suspicious. On the third day, she decided to test Filadoro. The ogress told the Prince to clean out the water tower which held a thousand barrels of water, saying that she wanted to fill it with fresh water. She added, if the job was not finished by dark, she would make mincemeat of him.

When the old woman went away Nardo Aniello began again to weep and wail once again. Filadoro, thinking her

107

mother a hard taskmaster, said to him, "Be quiet, and as soon as the stars are in proper alignment tonight we will be off."

The Prince, on hearing this news, embraced Filadoro and said, "You are my beacon of hope in this dark time."

When evening fell, Filadoro dug a hole in the garden leading into a long underground passage. Out they went, taking the road to Naples. When they reached the outskirts, the Prince said to Filadoro, "I cannot take you into the palace without a fine carriage and proper clothes. Wait for me at this inn, and I will soon return with horses, carriages, servants, and fine clothes."

So Filadoro stayed behind and the Prince went on his way to the city.

In the meantime, the ogress returned home, calling as usual for Filadoro to let down her hair. When there was no response, she knew immediately that something was wrong. She ran into the woods and cut a great, long pole and leaned it against the window, climbing up like a cat. Then she hunted everywhere inside the house and out. She looked high and low, but found no one. At last, she discovered the tunnel, and in her rage, tore out all her awful hair, cursing her daughter and the Prince. She prayed that the first time the Prince kissed anyone he would completely forget about Filadoro.

But let us leave the old woman for a moment and return to the Prince. On arriving at the palace, everyone in the whole house ran out to meet him, crying, "Welcome! Welcome! We thought you were dead, but here you are, safe and sound. How happy we are to see you back home." They showered him with a thousand words of affection.

Filadoro and the Dove

But as he was going up the stairs his mother met him halfway and embraced and kissed him, saying, "My son, my jewel, the apple of my eye, where have you been and why have you stayed away so long?"

The Prince didn't know what to say, because as soon as his mother kissed him—remember the curse of the ogress?—he forget where he had been. The Queen told her son to stop going out hunting and wasting his time in the woods. "I want you to get married," she said, "and settle down."

"Well and good," replied the Prince. "I am ready to do what you wish."

So it was settled that within four days he would marry a Princess from the far-off country of Flanders, and his mother set about planning a great wedding banquet.

Meanwhile, poor Filadoro waited at the inn. The days went by and the Prince never returned. She sat in the window and wept bitterly, as sad as a woman could be. As she was crying, a small white dove flew onto her shoulder. It was Filadoro's own pet dove, which she had saved from the clutches of a hawk, much like she had saved Nardo Aniello from the clutches of the ogress. The dove told Filadoro all about the curse and all about the wedding plans. Together, Filadoro and the dove made a plan to help the Prince recover his memory before he married the wrong princess.

Late that night, when everyone at the inn was fast asleep, Filadoro took the clothes of a servant boy, leaving her own in their place, and disguised herself as a man. Then she went to the back door of the palace where the cooks, needing extra help for the wedding festivities, took her in as a kitchen boy.

Filadoro and the Dove

When the tables were set and the guests all took their seats, the servants presented a large beautiful cake to the Princess of Flanders and Nardo Aniello. Filadoro had baked it with her own hands. When the carver cut the cake, out flew a beautiful white dove. The surprised guests forgot to eat and fell to admiring the pretty bird. The dove flew right up to the Prince and spoke to him in a pitiful voice. "How could you forget Filadoro and all the help she gave you, you ungrateful man? Is this how you repay the one who saved you from the claws of the ogress at the risk of her own life? Sad is the woman who trusts a man who pays his debts with ingratitude. But go, forget your promises. And may the curses follow you. The gods know the wrong you have done her, and when you least expect it, fever and illness will come to you. Unhappy Filadoro, deceived and forsaken, while you make merry with your new wife."

Then the dove flew away and vanished like the wind. The Prince stood for a moment, not knowing what to think. He asked the cake carver who had made the cake. The carver told him that a kitchen boy had made it, and ordered him to be brought into the room.

In came Filadoro, shedding a torrent of tears. The Prince at once remembered their vows and, instantly, lifted her in his arms and placed her by his side. Then he told his mother the whole story, of how the beautiful maiden had helped him, and how he must keep his promise to her.

"Do as you please," said his mother, "but you must not offend the Princess of Flanders who has come all this way to be your bride."

110

A cake was presented to the Princess of Flanders and Nardo Aniello.

Filadoro and the Dove

"Don't worry about me," said the Princess, "for to be honest I am homesick for my own parents and wish to return to my own country."

The Prince happily lifted a glass in a toast to the kind Princess and everyone in the banquet hall cheered her.

Then he ordered his servants to take away Filadoro's old clothes and bring her garments befitting a princess. Then the musicians began to play and the ball began, and the dancing lasted all night. At daybreak, the festivities finally ended, and everyone went home to rest. The Prince and Filadoro lived happily ever after, but he never went hunting again and he never again threw rocks at other people's pots, or caused trouble to others simply to amuse himself, proving that—

He who stumbles but does not fall,
Is helped on his way like a rolling ball.

Everyone in the banquet hall cheered Prince Nardo and Princess Filadoro.

THE MAN WITH THE GOLDEN HEAD

THERE was once a King of High Hill who longed for children more than pallbearers long for a funeral. At last his wife presented him with a little girl, whom they name Cannetella.

The child grew by leaps, and when she was as tall as a pole the King said to her, "My daughter, you are now grown up, and it is time to find you a husband worthy of you. Since I love you as my own life and desire to please you, tell me what sort of a husband you would like. What kind of a man would suit you? Will you have a scholar or a hunter? A boy, or an older man? Dark or fair? Tall as a maypole or short as a peg? Small in the chest or round as an ox? You choose, and I will be satisfied."

Cannetella thanked her father for his offer, but told him that she had no desire to marry. The King kept it up, however, urging her over and over again to choose a husband. Finally, Cannetella said, "I will comply with your wish if I can have a husband unlike any other in the world."

Her father, delighted beyond measure, sat at the window from morning till evening, looking out and examining every man that passed along the street. One day, seeing a good-looking young man go by, the King said to his daughter, "Run, Cannetella! See if he comes up to your standards."

The Man with the Golden Head

Cannetella invited the man in and they made a most splendid banquet for him. As they were eating an almond fell out of the youth's mouth; he quickly picked it up and put it under the tablecloth.

When they had done eating, the King said to Cannetella, "Well, my child, how does this youth please you?"

"Take the fellow away," said she. "A man so tall and so big should never let an almond drop out of his mouth." And so the young man was sent away.

The King returned to his seat at the window, and, presently, seeing another handsome young man pass by, he called his daughter to see if this one pleased her. Cannetella invited him to come in, and another banquet was made. And when they had done eating, and the man had gone away, the King asked his daughter whether he had pleased her. She replied, "What in the world would I do with such a miserable fellow who needs at least two servants just to take off his cloak?"

The King said, "It is plain that you are only making excuses and you have no intention of pleasing me. Make up your mind, for I will have you married."

To these angry words Cannetella replied, "To tell you the truth, dear father, I really feel that you are digging in the sea. I will never give myself to any man who does not have a golden head and teeth."

The poor King, seeing his daughter's determination, issued a proclamation, inviting anyone in his kingdom who could meet Cannetella's demands to appear, and he would give him both his daughter and the kingdom.

116

The Man with the Golden Head

Now this King had a mortal enemy named Fioravante, whom he could not bear the sight of. When Fioravante heard about this proclamation, he called his evil magicians to him, and commanded them to turn his head and teeth into gold. So they did as he desired, and when he saw himself with a head and teeth of pure gold he walked by the King's window. When the King saw the very man he was looking for, he called his daughter. As soon as Cannetella set eyes upon him she cried out, "He is the one! He could not be better if I had made him with my own hands."

As Fioravante continued walking, the King called out to him, "Wait, friend; don't be in such a hurry! One would think you had quicksilver in your body! Slow down, and I will give you my daughter and servants to go with her, for I wish her to be your wife."

"I thank you," said Fioravante, "but there is no need for servants; a single horse is enough to carry us both, for at my home I have as many servants as there are grains of sand at the seashore." After arguing awhile, Fioravante at last had his own way, and placing Cannetella behind him on a horse, he set out.

In the evening, they came to a stable where some horses were feeding. Fioravante led Cannetella into it and said, "Listen! I have to travel to my own house, and it will take me seven years to get there. Wait for me in this stable and do not go out, or let yourself be seen by any living person, or else I will punish you as long as you live." Cannetella replied, "You are my lord and master, and I will carry out your commands exactly. But tell me, what will I live on while I wait?"

The Man with the Golden Head

And Fioravante answered, "The leftovers from the horses' feed will be enough for you."

Imagine how poor Cannetella felt! Cold and hungry, what she lacked in food she made up for in tears. She bewailed her fate which had brought her down from a royal palace to a stable, from silken mattresses to a bed of straw, from delicious meals to the leftovers of horses.

She led this miserable life for several months. But one day, as she stood looking through a hole in the stable wall, she saw a most beautiful garden, in which groves of lemon trees and orange trees grew among beds of flowers and trellises of grape vines. This garden was a joy to behold! At the sight, Cannetella was seized by a great longing for a juicy bunch of grapes that caught her eye. She said to herself, "Come what may, even if the sky falls down, I will steal out softly and pluck it. What difference will it make a hundred years from now? There is no one here to tell on me. And even if my husband does hear about it, what can he do to me? Besides, these are very special grapes." So saying, she went out and indulged herself, eating all the grapes.

A little while later, and much sooner than she expected, her husband came back. One of his horses spoke up and told him all about Cannetella taking the grapes. At that, Fioravante in a rage drew his knife and was about to kill her. But, falling on her knees, Cannetella begged him to spare her, since hunger had driven her to it. She begged so hard that Fioravante replied, "I forgive you this time, but if you ever disobey me again, if you ever go outside and let the sun see you, I will make mincemeat of you. Now, listen to me: I am going away once more, and shall be gone for seven years. So take care, for you will not escape so easily again."

After he left, Cannetella shed a river of tears and, wringing her hands, beating her breast, and tearing her hair, she cried, "Oh, why was I born into the world to be doomed to such a wretched fate! Oh, Father, why did you make me marry? But why do I blame my father, when I myself chose my own husband? I caused my own misfortunes. This is my punishment, for I should have done what my father asked and not been so silly about finding a man with a gold head and gold teeth!"

And so she cried every day, until her eyes became two fountains, and her face was so thin and pale that her own father would not have recognized her.

At the end of one year the King's locksmith happened to pass by the stable. Cannetella called to him and went out to meet him. The smith heard his name, but did not recognize the poor girl, who was so thin and haggard. But when she told him her story, he said he would help her. He put her into an empty barrel tied to his pack horse and trotted off with her towards High Hill. At midnight he arrived at the King's palace, and knocked loudly on the door. At first the servants would not let him in, but the King, hearing the uproar, ordered the locksmith to be instantly admitted, for he knew that something unusual must have made him come at that hour. Then the smith, unloading his pack horse, knocked out the top of the barrel, and out tumbled Cannetella. If it hadn't been for a small brown mole on her arm her father would never have recognized her. But as soon as he saw it, he embraced and kissed her a thousand times. Then he instantly commanded a warm bath to be got ready for her, so she could bathe from head to foot and dress herself in her own clothes. Then he ordered food to be brought, for she was faint with hunger.

Then her father said, "Who has brought you to this sad condition?"

And she answered, "Alas, my dear sir, the man I chose has made me lead a dog's life, so that I was nearly at death's door. I cannot tell you what I have suffered, but now that I am home, I will never leave. I would rather be a servant in your house than a queen in another. I would rather be with you and wear rags, than be away from you and wear a golden cloak. I would rather cook in your kitchen, than sit on a throne somewhere else."

Meanwhile, when Fioravante returned home, the horses told him that the locksmith had carried off Cannetella in the barrel. On fire with rage, he ran off towards High Hill. There he met an old woman who lived in a tall house across the way from the palace. "How much will you charge, good woman, to let me up on your roof?"

When she asked for one hundred gold coins, Fioravante put his hand deep into his pocket and instantly counted out one hundred gold coins, one on top of the other. Then the old woman took him up on the roof, where he could see Cannetella drying her hair on a balcony across the way. Just as if her heart had whispered to her, the maiden turned and saw the evil man watching her. She rushed downstairs and ran to her

120

father, crying out, "My lord, if you do not this very instant lock the house with seven iron doors I am lost!"

"I will not lose you for such a trifle," said her father. "I would pluck out an eye to save you." So, no sooner said than done, and the iron doors were instantly made and locked tight.

When Fioravante saw the doors slam shut he went once more to the old woman and said to her, "Go to the King's house pretending to sell jars of rouge. Then make your way to the room of the King's daughter and when you get there, slip this little piece of paper under the bedcovers, and repeat these words—

'Let every one now soundly sleep,
But Cannetella awake shall keep.' "

For another hundred gold coins, the old woman agreed, and immediately carried out his orders.

As soon as she had done this trick, everyone in the house fell sound asleep, except for Cannetella who remained wide awake. When she heard the doors bursting open she cried out, but no one heard her, and no one ran to her aid. So, Fioravante broke down all seven doors and, entering her room, gathered up Cannetella, bedclothes and all, to carry her off. But, as luck would have it, the paper the old woman had put under the covers fell on the ground and, instantly, the spell was broken. Everyone in the house woke up and, hearing Cannetella's cries, they ran—cats, dogs, and all—to her aid. They caught the evil ogre and quickly cut him up in pieces like a

121

The Man with the Golden Head

tuna fish. Thus, he himself was caught in the trap he had laid for poor Cannetella, learning to his cost that—

No one suffers more pain
Than he who by his own sword is slain.

CORVETTO'S ADVENTURES IN
THE KING'S COURT

ONCE upon a time an excellent youth named Corvetto was in the service of the King of Wide River. For his good conduct he was beloved by his master; and for the same reason he was disliked by all the other courtiers. These comrades of his were filled with spite and malice, and bursting with envy at the kindness which the King showed to Corvetto. All day long, in every corner of the palace, they did nothing but whisper and grumble about the poor lad, saying, "What trick has this fellow played on the King that he takes such a fancy to him? How is he so lucky that every day he receives some new favor, while we are forever sliding backward, going from bad to worse, though we work like dogs, toil like laborers in the fields, and run about like deer to serve every whim of the King? Truly, one must be born lucky, and he who is not might as well be thrown into the sea. What can we do, but look on with envy?"

These words fell from their mouths like poisoned arrows aimed at Corvetto. Alas, in the Court, deceit and treachery weighed in by the ton! Who can count all the attempts these courtiers made to bring Corvetto to grief, or all the false tales they told about him to destroy his reputation! But Corvetto was enchanted, and was aware of all the tricks and traps they

123

set, and all the plots they planned against him. He kept his ears and eyes open in order not to take a false step, knowing that the fortune and good reputation of a courtier could easily be ruined. And the higher the lad rose in the Court, the lower the others fell. Since all their efforts had failed, the other courtiers thought they still might cause his downfall by using a very sneaky method known as flattery.

Ten miles away from the Court there lived an ogre, the most inhuman and savage that had ever been seen in Ogreland. The King had driven him away from the Court and now he lived in a lonesome wood on the top of a mountain, where no bird ever flew, and which was so thick and tangled with brush and vines that the sun never rose there. This ogre had a most beautiful horse which, among other wonderful things, could speak like any man. Now the courtiers, who knew how wicked the ogre was, how thick the woods, how high the mountain, and how difficult it was to get at the horse, went to the King and told him all about the beautiful horse and how it was worthy of a King. They added that he ought to save it from the ogre's claws, and that Corvetto was just the lad to do it, as he was the cleverest of them all. The King, who did not suspect that under the flowers of these words a snake was hiding, instantly called Corvetto, and said to him, "If you love me, try to capture for me the horse of my enemy, the ogre. You shall be well rewarded for doing me this service."

Corvetto knew about the plan cooked up by the other courtiers. Nevertheless, he obeyed the King and set out for the woods. When he reached the mountain top, he went very quietly into the stable, saddled and mounted the horse, and placing his feet firmly in the stirrups, began the journey back. But as soon as the horse saw himself being ridden away, he cried aloud, "Look out! Corvetto is riding off with me."

At this alarm, the ogre instantly ran out, with all the dogs and other animals that served him, to cut Corvetto to pieces. From one side jumped an ape, from the other came a large bear; here sprang forth a lion, there came running a wolf. But Corvetto, digging in his spurs, put the woods behind him, and galloped without stop back to the Court, where he presented the horse to the King.

Then the King embraced him like a son, and pulling out his purse, filled his hands with gold pieces. Now the courtiers were furious. Where before they were a little steamed up, now they were bursting with hot anger. The crowbar with which they had expected to smash Corvetto's good fortune had only served to smooth his path. Knowing, however, that walls are not broken down by the first attack of the battering ram, they decided to try again. This time they said to the King, "We hope you enjoy the beautiful horse! It will indeed be an ornament to the royal stable. But what a shame you don't have the ogre's fabulous tapestries that hang on all the walls of his castle and cover every bed and table, cloths more beautiful than words can tell. To own them would spread your fame far and wide! No one can procure these treasures but Corvetto, who is just the lad to do this difficult service."

Then the King, who danced to every tune these rogues played, called Corvetto, and begged him to procure for him the ogre's tapestries. Off went Corvetto, and no sooner was he on the top of the mountain than he passed unseen into the bed chamber where the ogre slept. There he hid himself under the bed, and waited as still as a mouse, until the ogre and his wife went to bed. Then Corvetto quietly stripped the tapestries off the walls and began to gently pull the silken cover off the bed. The ogre suddenly awoke and told his wife to stop dragging all the bedclothes off him, for he would catch his death of cold.

"Why, you are the one who is uncovering me!" answered the ogress.

"Where is the bedcover?" asked the ogre. Stretching out his hand in the dark he touched Corvetto's face. The ogre cried out, "The imp! The imp! Lights! Come quickly!" The whole house was turned topsy-turvy with the noise as all the ogre's servants came running. But Corvetto threw the tapestries out of the window and jumped out on top of them. Then gathering them up into a big bundle he set out down the road to the Court.

You cannot imagine how pleased the King was to see him; nor can you imagine how bursting with spite were the courtiers. Nevertheless, they laid on one more devious plan. They went again to the King, who was beside himself with delight at the tapestries which were all silk embroidered with gold, with glittering jewels sewn into them, telling elaborate stories with pictures and words woven into the fabric.

The courtiers came to the King and said, "As Corvetto has done so much to serve you, it would be nothing for him to get the ogre's palace, which is fit for an emperor to live in. It has so many rooms that it can hold an army. And you would never believe all the courtyards, staircases, balconies, and chimneys which are there—built with such marvelous architecture that it puts both art and nature to shame."

The King, who was eager to have all of the ogre's wealth, called Corvetto again. This time he described how he longed for the ogre's palace, and begged him to add this service to all the others he had done for him. So Corvetto instantly set out again. When he arrived at the ogre's palace, the ogre was out inviting all his relatives over for dinner. Corvetto found the ogress alone in the kitchen busy preparing a feast. Corvetto entered with a look of compassion and said, "Good day, my good woman! Truly, you are a brave woman! Only yesterday you were ill in bed, and now you are working so hard in the kitchen."

"What can I do?" replied the ogress. "I have no one to help me."

"I am here," answered Corvetto, "ready to help you."

"Welcome then!" said the ogress. "Since you are so kind, just help me to split four logs of wood."

"With all my heart," answered Corvetto. "But if four logs are not enough, let me split five."

And, taking up a newly ground axe, instead of striking the wood, he struck the ogress on the neck, and she fell down like a pear falling from a tree. Then, running quickly to the gate, Corvetto dug a deep hole before the entrance, and covered it over with bushes and earth. Then he hid himself in the shadows.

As soon as Corvetto saw the ogre coming home with all his kinfolk, he set up a loud cry in the courtyard: "Stop, stop! I have caught him! Long live the King of Wide River."

Corvetto's Adventures in the King's Court

When the ogre heard this challenge, he ran like mad at Corvetto. But as he rushed furiously towards the gate, he tumbled head over heels down into the pit and all of his relatives with him, where Corvetto speedily stoned them to death.

Then Corvetto locked the door of the ogre's palace and took the keys to the King. Seeing the bravery and cleverness of the lad, the King's daughter chose him for her husband. The envy of the courtiers had only launched Corvetto's ship of life on the sea of greatness. That night, while his enemies wept with rage, Corvetto went peacefully to bed, for—

> *Punishment for ill deeds past*
> *May be delayed, but comes at last.*

THE BOOBY WHO FOOLED
A WISE MAN

THERE once was a man who was as rich as the sea, but as there can never be any perfect happiness in this world, he had a son so idle and good-for-nothing that he did not know the difference between a bean and a cucumber. At last, being tired of his foolishness, he gave his son a good handful of coins and sent him to a faraway country to buy goods for the household, hoping that seeing various countries and meeting different people would awaken his mind and sharpen his judgment.

Moscione (for that was the name of the son) got up on his horse and began his journey towards Venice, the center of all the wonders of the world. From there, he embarked on board a ship bound for Cairo. When he reached Egyptian shores, he set off again on foot. When he had traveled a good day's journey, he met a young man who was standing beneath the shade of a poplar tree. Moscione asked, "What is your name, my lad? And what is your trade?"

And the lad replied, "My name is Lightning; I am from Arrowland, and I can run like the wind."

"I should like to see you prove it," said Moscione.

And Lightning answered, "Wait a moment, and you will see whether what I say is dust or flour."

The Booby Who Fooled a Wise Man

After they had stood waiting a little while, a doe came bounding over the plain. Lighting let her pass, to give her a good head start, then darted after her so rapidly and light of foot that he could have run across a field of flour without leaving a mark of his shoe. In only four bounds he had caught up with her. Moscione, amazed at this exploit, asked if Lightning would come and live with him, and promised to pay him royally.

So Lightning consented, and they went on their way together. But they had not gone very far when they met another young man. Moscione asked, "What is your name, friend? What country are you from? And what is your trade?"

"My name is Quick Ear," replied the lad. "I am from Curious Valley. And when I put my ear to the ground, I can hear everything that is happening in the world without moving from the spot. I learn all the business going on, the prices of goods, the deceitfulness of courtiers, the plans of lovers, the plots of robbers, the reports of spies, the complaints of servants, the gossiping of old women, and the oaths of sailors. No one has ever been able to learn as much as my ears can."

"If that be true," said Moscione, "tell me what they are saying now at my home."

So the lad put his ear to the ground, and replied, "An old man is talking to his wife, and saying, 'Praised be! I have got rid of that fellow Moscione. By traveling through the world he will at least become a man, and no longer be such a stupid donkey, such a simpleton, such a lazy fellow, such a —— '"

"Stop, stop!" cried Moscione. "You tell the truth and I

believe you. So come along with me, for you have found the road to good luck."

"Well and good!" said the youth. So they all went on together and traveled ten miles farther, when they met another young man, to whom Moscione said, "What is your name, my brave fellow? Where were you born? And what can you do in the world?"

And the man answered, "My name is Shoot Straight. I am from Castle Aim Well, and with a crossbow I can shoot so point-blank that I can split the smallest crab apple down the middle."

"I should like to see the proof," said Moscione.

So the lad loaded his crossbow, took aim, and made a pea leap from the top of a stone. At that expert performance, Moscione took him also into his company of men. And they all four traveled on another day's journey, till they came to a group of workers who were building a large pier in the scorching heat of the sun. Moscione said, "My friends, how can you work in this furnace, which is fit to roast a buffalo?"

And one of the builders answered, "Oh, we are as cool as a rose. For we have a young man here who blows upon us as if the west wind were blowing."

"Let me see him, please," cried Moscione.

So the worker called the lad, and Moscione said to him, "Tell me, what is your name? What country are you from? And what is your profession?"

And the lad replied, "My name is Blow Blast. I am from Windy Land, and I can make all the winds with my mouth. If you wish for a sea breeze, I will breathe one that will send your ship speedily along its course. If you wish for a squall, I will throw down houses."

"Seeing is believing," said Moscione. At his words, Blow Blast breathed quite gently, so that it seemed to be the wind that blows at Posilippo towards evening. Then, turning suddenly to some trees, he sent forth such a furious blast that it uprooted a row of oaks.

When Moscione saw this he took him for a companion. And traveling on again, he met another lad, to whom he said, "What is your name, if I may make so bold? Where do you come from? And what is your trade, if I may ask?"

And the lad answered, "My name is Strong Back. I am from Valentino, and I am so strong that I can lift a mountain on my back, and it feels like a feather."

"If that's the case," said Moscione, "you deserve to be the king of the treasury, and you should carry our flag in the May Day parade. But I should like to see a proof of what you say."

Then Strong Back began to load onto his back masses of rock, trunks of trees, and so many other weights that a thousand large wagons could not have carried them. When Moscione saw this feat, he asked the lad to join them.

So they traveled on till they came to Fair Flower, where lived a Princess who ran like the wind, and could pass over the waving corn without bending an ear. Her father, the King, who had no intention of giving his daughter in marriage to anyone, but quite enjoyed watching foot races, had issued a proclamation that whoever could outrun her should have her for a wife, but whoever was left behind should lose his head.

When Moscione heard the proclamation, he went straight

The Booby Who Fooled a Wise Man

to the King, and offered to run with his daughter, agreeing that he would either win the race or leave his head there. But in the morning he sent a message to the King saying that he was taken ill and, being unable to run himself, he would send another young man in his place.

"Come who will!" said the Princess, whose name was Ciannetella. "I care not a fig—it is all the same to me."

Soon, the great square of the city was filled with people who had come to see the race. It was so crowded that people swarmed like ants, and hung from the windows and rooftops. Lightning came out and took his place at the top of the square, waiting for the signal.

And then came Ciannetella, dressed in a little gown, tucked halfway up her legs, wearing pretty little sandals tied neatly to her feet. The two runners stood shoulder to shoulder, and as soon as the sound of the trumpets was heard, off they darted, running so fast that their heels touched their shoulders. They ran as fast as rabbits with the greyhounds chasing them, as horses broken loose from the stable, or as dogs with kettles tied to their tails. But Lightning left the princess more than a half foot behind him, and came first to the finish line.

You should have heard the shouting and the uproar, the whistling and clapping of hands as all the people cried out, "Hurrah! Long live the stranger!"

Ciannetella's face turned as red as a schoolboy's who is going to be punished, and she stood lost in shame and confusion.

But it was not over yet. There was one more heat to the race. She began to plan her revenge. She put a magic charm into a ring with such power that if anyone put the ring on his finger his legs would totter so that he would be unable to walk, much less run. Then she sent the ring as a present to Lightning, begging him to wear it on his finger for love of her.

Quick Ear heard her tell her father about the trick, but decided to say nothing for the time being. When they returned to the field for the second race, they took up their positions as before. With the blare of the trumpets Ciannetella was off, like another Atalanta. But Lightning was like an old donkey, for he could not stir a step.

Shoot Straight saw his comrade's danger, and heard from Quick Ear about the ring. He picked up his crossbow and shot an arrow so exactly that it hit Lightning's finger, and out flew the charm from the ring. Lightning's legs were set free, and with four goat-leaps he passed Ciannetella and won the race.

The King saw that a blockhead had outwitted him and beaten his daughter. He had no wish to see his prize carried off by a fool. So thinking, he consulted with his councillors, who agreed that Ciannetella was not a mouthful for the tooth of such a miserable dog. They suggested that the King could properly go back on his promise by giving Moscione gold coins instead, which he would probably like better than all the women in the world.

This advice pleased the King, and he asked Moscione how much money he would take instead of the Princess who had been promised him.

Moscione, after consulting with his comrades, answered, "I

will take as much gold and silver as one of my friends can carry on his back."

The King agreed. And then the lads presented Strong Back, on whom they began to load bales of gold, sacks of silver, large purses full of coins, barrels of copper money, chests full of rings. The more they loaded him the firmer he stood, just like a tower, so that the treasury, the banks, and all the money-dealers of the city were not enough to fill him up. The King sent messages to all the great people in every direction to borrow their silver candlesticks, bowls, jugs, plates, trays, and baskets. And yet even all this was not enough to load him up. At last, Moscione and his friends went on their way, not completely filled up, but tired and satisfied.

When the councillors saw what heaps of wealth these six miserable dogs were carrying off, they said to the King that it was a great piece of donkeyhood to let them take away the life's blood of the kingdom. Why not send troops after them to lessen the load of that Atlas who was carrying on his shoulders a heaven of treasure?

The King listened to this advice, and immediately dispatched a party of armed men, on foot and on horseback, to overtake Moscione and his friends. But Quick Ear, who had heard all about the plan, told his comrades. While the dust was rising up from the trampling of the army who were coming fast to unload the rich cargo, Blow Blast began to blow so hard that he not only made the enemies fall flat on the ground, but also sent them flying for miles just like a tornado does. And that was the end of that story. When Moscione arrived back at his father's house, he shared the booty with his companions, and sent them away content and happy. He himself stayed with his father, rich beyond measure, and saw himself, a mere blockhead, laden with gold, proving the old saying—

Heaven sends pudding to him who has no teeth.

THE STONE IN THE COCK'S HEAD

THERE once lived in the city of Dark Grotto a certain man named Minecco Aniello, whose luck was so bad that he possessed only a short-legged cock, which he fed breadcrumbs. But one morning, being pinched with appetite, he decided to sell the cock. Taking it to the market, he met two thievish magicians, with whom he made a bargain, and sold it for one silver coin. They told Minecco Aniello to take the cock to their house, and they would count him out the money. Then the magicians went on their way. Minecco Aniello overheard them whispering excitedly together and saying, "Who could believe that we would meet with such good luck, Jennarone? This cock will make our fortune with the stone which, you know, he has in his head. We will have it set in a ring, and then we shall have everything we want."

"Be quiet, Jacovuccio," answered his friend. "I see myself rich and can hardly believe it. I am longing to twist the cock's neck and give a kick to the face of beggary. For in this world, virtue without money is worthless, and a man is judged by the clothes he wears."

When Minecco Aniello, who was worldly wise (oh yes, he had traveled about in the world and eaten bread from more than one oven), heard their whispers he turned on his heel and

137

The Stone in the Cock's Head

scampered off. Running home, he twisted the cock's neck, and split open its head. Inside he found the prized stone, which he took to the ringmaker to be set in a brass ring. Holding the ring in the palm of his hand, he tested its powers, saying out loud, "I wish to become a youth eighteen years old."

Hardly had he uttered the words when his blood began to flow more quickly, his nerves became stronger, his limbs firmer, his flesh fresher, his eyes more fiery, his silver hairs were turned into gold, his mouth, which was an empty village, became peopled with teeth; his beard, which was as thick as a forest, became like a nursery garden—in short, he was changed to a most beautiful young man.

Then he said again, "I wish for a splendid palace, and to marry the King's daughter."

And, lo! There instantly appeared a magnificent palace in which were rooms that would amaze you, columns to astound you, pictures to fill you with wonder; silver glittered all around, and gold was hard underfoot; the jewels dazzled your eyes; the servants swarmed like ants, the horses and carriages were countless—in short, there was such a display of riches that the King himself stared at the sight, and willingly gave Minecco Aniello the hand of his daughter Natalizia.

Meanwhile, the magicians, having discovered Minecco Aniello's great wealth, planned to steal his good fortune. They made a pretty little doll which played and danced when wound up. Then dressing themselves like merchants, they went to Pentella, the daughter of Minecco Aniello, and offered to sell the doll to her. When Pentella asked the price, they replied that it could not be bought for money, but that she might have it for nothing if she would only do them a favor.

"What favor is that?" the little girl asked.

"Let us see your father's ring that we might make a model of it. Then you can have the doll in exchange."

Pentella, who had never heard the old saying, "Think before you buy anything cheap," instantly accepted this offer. She promised to ask her father to lend her the ring and told the two false merchants to return the next morning. When her father returned home Pentella coaxed and caressed him, until at last she persuaded him to give her the ring, saying that she was sad at heart, and wished to amuse herself a little.

Early the next morning, as soon as the sun swept the last trace of shadows from the streets, the magicians returned, and no sooner did Pentella place the ring in their hands than they instantly vanished, and not a trace of them was to be seen. Poor Pentella nearly died with terror.

When the magicians came to a wood, where the branches of some of the trees were dancing like swords, they asked the ring to destroy the spell by which the old man had become young again. And instantly Minecco Aniello, who was at that moment standing tall and handsome beside the King, suddenly turned old, his golden hair grew white, his forehead wrinkled, his eyebrows grew bristly, his eyes sunk in their sockets, his mouth lost its teeth, his beard grew bushy, his back grew a hump, his legs trembled, and, above all, his glittering garments turned to rags and tatters.

The King, seeing now a miserable beggar standing beside him, ordered him to be instantly driven away with blows and

The Stone in the Cock's Head

hard words. Aniello, thus suddenly fallen from his good luck, went weeping to his daughter, and asked her for the ring so that he could set matters to rights again. But when he heard about the fatal trick played by the false merchants he was ready to throw himself from the window, cursing the ignorance of his daughter, who, for the sake of a silly doll had turned him into a miserable scarecrow. He was determined to go wandering about the world like a bad penny, until he found those merchants who had robbed him.

So saying, he threw a cloak about his shoulders, and a knapsack on his back, took a staff in his hand, and, leaving his daughter behind, he set out walking desperately on and on.

Eventually, he arrived at the kingdom of Deep Hole, inhabited by mice. The mice thought he was out spying for the cats, and instantly led him before their King, Rosecone.

"Who are you? Where do you come from? And why are you here?" the King asked.

Minecco Aniello presented the Mouse King with a piece of cheese as a gift, then told him all about his misfortune. He concluded by saying that he would continue his travels, until he found those villains who had robbed him of so precious a jewel, taking from him at once the flower of his youth, the source of his wealth, and the proof of his honor.

At these words, Rosecone felt pity nibbling at his heart. Wishing to comfort the poor man, he summoned his council of old mice and asked for their advice, commanding them to use all their resources to gather news of the whereabouts of false merchants. Now, among the elder mice were present Rudolo and Saltariello, two mice who knew the ways of the

140

world, for they had lived for six years at a tavern of a great resort nearby. They said to Minecco Aniello, "Be of good heart, comrade! Things will turn out better than you imagine. One day, when we were in a room at the tavern where the most famous men in the world make merry, two men from far-off Hook Castle came in to eat and drink. After they had eaten their fill and had seen the bottom of their bottle, they began to talk about a trick they had played on a certain old man of Dark Grotto, and how they had cheated him out of a stone of great value. One of them, named Jennarone, said he would never take the stone from his finger, so he would never lose it as the old man's daughter had done."

When Minecco Aniello heard this, he asked the two mice if they would accompany him to the country where these rogues lived and recover the ring for him. He offered to give them a big lot of cheese and salt meat, which they might eat and enjoy with the King. Then the two mice, after bargaining a little for the reward, agreed to go over sea and mountain and, taking leave of his mousy majesty, they set out.

After journeying a long way they arrived at Hook Castle. There the mice told Minecco Aniello to hide under some trees on the banks of the river. Then they went to find the house of the merchants. They easily located the dwelling and set up a watch, observing all the comings and goings of the two men. When they saw that Jennarone never took the ring from his finger, they hatched a plot between them. Waiting till Night had dyed purple the sunburnt face of Heaven, and the magicians had gone to bed and were fast asleep, the two mice tiptoed into their bed chamber. Rudolo began to nibble the finger on which the ring was. Jennarone, feeling the tingle, took the ring off and laid it on a table beside the bed. As soon as Saltariello saw this, he popped the ring into his mouth, and in four skips he was off, with Rudolo scampering after him.

The two elderly mice, having as much fun as little mice playing tricks, ran back to Minecco Aniello and delivered the ring right into his hand. The old man, happier than a man at the gallows feels when a pardon arrives, put the ring on his finger and instantly turned the magicians into two jackasses. Then, throwing his cloak over one of them, he rode him like a noble count. He loaded the other with cheese and bacon, and set off toward Deep Hole, where he gave presents to the Mouse King and his mouse councillors, thanking them for all the good fortune he had received by their help, praying to Heaven that no mousetrap might ever catch them, that no cat might ever harm them, and that no poison might ever poison them.

Then, leaving the kingdom of the mice, Minecco Aniello returned to Dark Grotto, more handsome than before, and was received by the King and his daughter with the greatest affection in the world. He lived happily ever after, never again taking the ring from his finger, having learned his lesson, for—

The cat who has been burned with fire
ever after fears the stove.

Minecco Aniello Meeting the Magicians
Page 137

Rita Riding on the Giant Fish
Page 144

THE THREE ENCHANTED PRINCES

ONCE upon a time the King of Green Bank had three daughters, who were perfect jewels. The three sons of the King of Fair Meadow were desperately in love with them, but these princes had been changed into animals by the spell of a fairy. The King of Green Bank did not want his daughters to marry them. The first Prince, who was a beautiful Falcon, called together all the other birds to advise him; there came the finches, the woodpeckers, the flycatchers, jays, blackbirds, cuckoos, thrushes, and every other kind of bird. When they were all assembled before the Prince, he ordered them to destroy all the blossoms on the trees, so that not a flower or leaf remained.

The second Prince, who was a Stag, summoned all the goats, rabbits, hares, hedgehogs, and other animals of that country, and told them to destroy all the cornfields, so that there was not a single blade of grass or corn left.

The third Prince, who was a Fish, consulted together with a hundred sea creatures and made such a storm arise upon that coastline that every boat was sunk.

Now the King saw how matters were going from bad to worse, and knew he could not stop the mischief made by these three wild lovers. So he made up his mind to agree that his daughters might marry them. With feasts and dancing, the

143

three princes married their brides and carried them out of the kingdom.

The Queen, Granzolla, gave each of her daughters a ring, all exactly alike, telling them that if they happened to be separated, and meet again years later, or to see any of their relatives, they would recognize one another by these rings.

So taking their leave the three couples departed. The Falcon carried Fabiella, who was the eldest of the sisters, to the top of a mountain, which was so high that it passed the clouds into the dry air where it never rains. There, he lead her to a most beautiful palace, where she lived like a queen.

The Stag carried Vasta, the second sister, into a wood, which was so thick that not even the Shades could find their way to escort her. There he placed her, as befitted her rank, in a wonderfully splendid house with a garden.

The Fish swam with Rita, the third sister, on his back into the middle of the sea. There, upon a large rock, he showed her a mansion big enough for three kings.

Meanwhile, back in Green Bank, Granzolla gave birth to a fine little boy, whom they named Tittone. When he was fifteen years old, hearing his mother complain that she never heard any news of her three daughters, who were married to three animals, he decided to go looking for them. After he begged his father and mother for a long time, they granted him permission to go traveling through the world in search of his sisters, bidding him take along attendants and everything a Prince might need. The Queen also gave him another ring similar to those she had given to her daughters.

Tittone went on his way, searching every corner of Italy,

every nook in France, and every part of Spain. Then he passed through England and visited Poland. In short, he traveled both east and west, north and south. At last, he ran out of money. Leaving all his servants, some at the taverns and some at the hospitals, he set out without a penny in his pocket. Finally, he came to the top of the mountain where the Falcon and Fabiella lived. And as he stood there, contemplating the beauty of the palace—the walls of marble, the windows of gold, and the tiles of silver—his sister saw him, and ordered him brought before her.

"Who are you?" she asked. "Where do you come from? And why are you here?"

When Tittone told her the name of his country, the name of his father and mother, and his own name, Fabiella knew that he was her brother. When she compared the ring upon his finger with her own ring she embraced him with great joy. But she hid him in a closet, fearing that her husband would be angry when he returned home.

As soon as the Falcon came home, Fabiella began to tell him that she was lonely for her parents. The Falcon answered, "It's impossible for you to go home now."

"Can we at least send for one of my relatives to keep me company?" asked Fabiella.

"But, who will come so far to see you?" replied the Falcon.

"If anyone should come," asked Fabiella, "would you be displeased?"

"Why should I be displeased?" said the Falcon. "If he were one of your relatives I would take him to my heart."

The Three Enchanted Princes

When Fabiella heard this she took courage, and called for Tittone to come out. She presented him to the Falcon, who exclaimed, "Five and five are ten; water passed through the strongest boot. A hearty welcome to you! You are master in this house. Ask for whatever you want, and do whatever you like." Then he gave orders that Tittone should be served and treated with the same honor as himself.

Now when Tittone had stayed two weeks on the mountain, he decided to go forth and seek his other sisters. The Falcon gave him one of his feathers, saying, "Take this and prize it, my dear Tittone; for one day you may need it. Take good care of it; and if ever you meet with any trouble, throw it on the ground, and say, 'Come hither, come hither!' and you shall have cause to thank me."

Tittone wrapped the feather up in tissue paper and put it in his pocket. After a thousand ceremonies he departed, traveling on and on a very long way. He arrived at last at the forest where the Stag lived with Vasta. Going half-dead with hunger into the garden, he plucked some fruit. His sister saw him there, and recognized him in the same manner as Fabiella had done. Then she presented Tittone to her husband, who received him with the greatest friendship, and treated him truly like a prince.

At the end of two weeks, Tittone decided to depart, and go in search of his other sister. The Stag gave him one of his hairs, repeating the same words as the Falcon had spoken about the feather. And setting out on his way, with a bagful of gold pieces which the Falcon had given him, and as many more which the Stag gave him, he walked on and on, until he came to the end of the earth, where he was stopped by the sea. Unable to walk any farther, he boarded a ship, intending to search all the islands for news of his sister. He sailed all about, until at last he was carried to an island where lived the Fish with Rita. No sooner had he landed, than his sister saw and recognized him in the same manner as the others had done, and he was received by her husband with all possible affection.

Now after a while Tittone wished to set out again to go home to his father and mother, whom he had not seen for so long a time. The Fish gave him one of his scales, telling him the same as the Stag and the Falcon had. Tittone, sailed back to the mainland, mounted a horse, and set out on his travels. But he had hardly gone half a mile from the seashore, when entering a wood—the abode of Fear where continual darkness and terror was kept up—he saw a great tower rising up in the middle of a lake. At a window in the tower Tittone saw a most beautiful maiden sitting at the feet of a hideous dragon, who was asleep. When the damsel saw Tittone, she whispered in a low voice, "O noble youth, are you here to release me from the power of this tyrannical serpent, who has carried me off from my father, the King of Bright Valley, and shut me up in this frightful tower?"

"Alas, my beautiful lady!" replied Tittone. "What can I do to help thee? Who can pass this lake? Who can climb this tower? Who can get near that horrid dragon, that carries terror in his eyes, and sows fear everywhere? But wait a minute. We'll find a way to drive this serpent away. Carefully, step by step— the more haste, the less speed." And so saying, he threw the feather, the hair, and the scale, which his brothers-in-law had given him, on the ground, exclaiming, "Come hither, come hither!"

And dropping to the earth like drops of summer rain suddenly there appeared the Falcon, the Stag, and the Fish, who cried out all together, "Behold us here! What are your commands?"

When Tittone saw them, he said with great joy, "I wish only to release this poor maiden from the claws of yon dragon, to take her away from this tower, to destroy it, and to carry this beautiful lady home with me as my wife."

"Say no more!" answered the Falcon. "We'll soon make him dance upon a penny."

"Let's hurry," said the Stag. "Troubles and macaroni are best when swallowed hot."

So the Falcon summoned a large flock of griffins, who as you know have the wings of an eagle and the body of a lion, who flew to the window of the tower and carried off the damsel. They flew with her over the lake and set her down right where Tittone was standing with his three brothers-in-law. If she had looked like the moon before, believe me, up close she was as beautiful as the sun.

While Tittone was embracing her and telling her how he loved her, the dragon awoke. Rushing out of the window, he came swimming across the lake to swallow up Tittone. But the Stag instantly called up a squadron of lions, tigers, panthers, bears, and wild cats, who fell upon the dragon and tore him to pieces with their claws. Tittone was ready to leave with the maiden, when the Fish said, "I also wish to do something for you." And he made the sea rise so high that it swept over the evil tower, throwing it down to its very foundation.

When Tittone saw all of these good deeds, he thanked the animals in the best manner he could, telling the damsel that they were the ones who had saved her.

But the animals answered, "We are the ones who are grateful, for this beautiful lady can restore us to our proper shapes. Before we were born, our mother offended a magician. At our birth, he laid a spell on us and we were compelled to remain in the form of animals until we had freed the daughter of a king from some great trouble. Now the time has come which we have waited for. The fruit is ripe, and we already feel a new spirit in our breasts, new blood in our veins."

So saying, they were changed into three handsome youths, and one after another they embraced their brother-in-law, and shook hands with the lady, who was overjoyed.

When Tittone saw this, he nearly fainted dead away. "O Heavens!" he said. "If only my mother and father could share in this happiness! They would be so glad to see such graceful and handsome sons-in-law before their eyes."

Answered the princes, "Until now, the shame at seeing ourselves transformed into animals made us hide from others. But now we can appear in the world again. We will all go and live with our wives under one roof, and spend our lives merrily. Let us go instantly, and before the sun rises we and our wives shall be with you at your home."

All they had to ride on was Tittone's horse, so the three princes caused a most beautiful coach to appear, drawn by six lions, in which they all five seated themselves. Having traveled

The Three Enchanted Princes

the whole day, they came in the evening to a tavern where they had supper and read all the silly messages other men had scribbled on the wall, for, yes, even in those days graffiti was common proof of ignorance. After everyone had eaten their fill and retired to rest, the three princes went out and walked about the whole night long. In the morning, when the stars, like bashful maidens, retired from the gaze of the sun, they found their wives and brought them back to the tavern just as the sun rose. There was a great embracing, and joy beyond measure. Then they all eight seated themselves in the same coach, and made their way on to Green Bank, where they were received with incredible affection by the King and Queen. Not only had the parents regained their four children, whom they had considered lost, but they also gained three sons-in-law and a daughter-in-law. When the news of the adventures of their children was heard by the kings of Fair Meadow and Bright Valley, they came to Green Bank to see their children and all the families shared their happiness together, each adding a rich ingredient of joy to the porridge of their satisfaction, and receiving full compensation for all their past misfortunes; for—

One hour of joy dispels
the cares and sufferings of a thousand years.

THE DRAGONSLAYER

THERE was one time a King of High Shore, who was so cruel that while he was away on a trip his royal throne was taken over by a certain sorceress. The King was furious when he learned he had lost his throne. He asked the advice of a wooden statue that was known to give answers to serious problems, and the statue told him he could recover his kingdom when the sorceress lost her sight. The King was eager to kill the sorceress, but she was well protected by her guards. He became so desperate, that out of spite to her, he killed all the women in the country whom he could capture.

After hundreds and hundreds had lost their lives, the next in line was a maiden named Porziella, the most beautiful creature on the whole earth. She was so beautiful the King could not help falling in love with her and making her his wife. But he was so cruel and spiteful to women that, after a while, he decided to kill her like the rest. Just as he was raising the dagger, a little bird dropped a twig upon his arm, and the King began to tremble so hard that the weapon fell from his hand.

This bird was really a fairy, who, a few days before, having gone to sleep in a wood, was about to be robbed by a wood satyr, who, as you know, is half man and half goat. Just in time, Porziella found the fairy and woke her up before the satyr could steal her treasure, which in her case were all her magic secrets. For this kindness, the fairy always followed Porziella's steps to protect her.

When the King saw this, he thought that the beauty of Porziella's face had stopped his arm and bewitched the dagger. He decided not to try again, but instead he would seal her up tight in a garret and leave her there until she starved to death. No sooner said than done: the unhappy girl was enclosed within four walls, without having anything to eat or drink, and left to waste away and die little by little.

The bird, seeing her in this wretched state, consoled her with kind words. Then, bidding her be of good cheer, the bird promised to return the great kindness Porziella had done for her, and to help her even if she had to give up her own life. The bird would never tell Porziella who she was, only that she owed her a great debt and would leave nothing undone to serve her.

Seeing that the poor girl was famished with hunger, the bird flew away and quickly returned with a sharp knife from the king's pantry; she told Porziella to dig a hole in the corner of the floor, which was just above the kitchen. Through the hole the bird would regularly bring her food to sustain her life. So Porziella bored away until she had made a passage for the bird, who, watching till the cook went out to fetch a pitcher of water from the well, flew down through the hole and taking a fine chicken that was roasting over the fire, brought it to Porziella. Not knowing how to carry any water, the bird flew to the arbor and selected a fine bunch of grapes for Porziella to eat. The bird continued to make these trips day after day.

After several months had passed, Porziella gave birth to a

fine little boy, whom she reared with the constant help of the bird. And when he was grown big, the bird advised her to lift up the floor boards so that Miuccio (for that was the child's name) could pass through. So Porziella did as the bird directed her. And as soon as the cook had gone out, she let down her son through the opening, using a cord the bird had brought. Then she put the floor boards back into place, so no one would know where he came from. She warned him never to tell whose son he was.

When the cook returned and saw such a fine little boy standing in the kitchen, he asked him who he was, where he came from, and what he wanted. The child, remembering his mother's advice, said that he was a poor, forlorn boy who was looking for a master. As they were talking, the butler came in, and seeing the spritely little fellow, he thought he would make a pretty page for the King. So he led him to the royal apartments. When the King saw him looking as handsome as a jewel, he was very pleased with him, and took him into his service as a page, and into his heart as a son. The King taught him all the skills of a cavalier, so that Miuccio grew up the most accomplished boy in the court, and the King loved him much better than his stepbrother, who was next in line for the throne. Now the King's stepmother, who was really the Queen, began to take a dislike to Miuccio. The more favors and kindnesses the King bestowed on him, the greater her envy and malice grew. She decided to grease the ladder of his fortune so that he would tumble down from top to bottom.

Accordingly, one evening, the old Queen told the King that Miuccio had boasted he would build three castles in the

The Dragonslayer

air. So the next morning, the King, to gratify his stepmother, ordered Miuccio to be called, and commanded him to build the three castles in the air as he had promised, or else he would make him dance a jig in the air.

When Miuccio heard this he went to his room and began to weep. His good luck had run out already! While he was crying, the bird came, and said to him, "Take heart, Miuccio, and fear not while I am by your side, for I can help you." Then she told him to take cardboard and glue and make three large paper castles. She called up three large griffins, which have the body of a lion, and the wings of eagles; she tied a castle to each one and away they flew up into the air.

Miuccio called the King, who came running with all his court to see the sight. When he saw the cleverness of Miuccio he liked him better than ever, and lavished all kinds of praise upon him. The old Queen was more envious than before. Seeing her plan fail, she plotted day and night to get rid of Miuccio. At last, after some days, she said to the King, "Son, the time has come for us to return to our former greatness and the pleasures of past times. Miuccio has offered to blind the sorceress, and make you recover your lost kingdom."

The King, who was touched in his sore spot, called for Miuccio that very instant, and said to him, "I am greatly surprised to learn that that you have the power to restore my kingdom and haven't told me so. Here I am, reduced from a kingdom to a little farm, from a great city to a paltry castle, and from commanding an army to being waited on by a handful of servants. If you love me, run now at once and blind the eyes of the sorceress who keeps my property. By putting out her lanterns you will light the lamps of my honor that are now dark and dismal."

When Miuccio heard this request he was about to reply that the King had the wrong idea. He was neither a raven to pick out eyes nor an drill to bore holes. But the King said, "No more words—so I will have it, so let it be done! Remember now, that in the treasury of my brain I keep the accounts balanced. In one scale is the reward, if you do what I tell you. In the other, the punishment, if you fail."

Miuccio, who saw there was no point butting his head against a rock, went into a corner to bemoan his terrible fate. The bird came to him and said, "Is it possible, Miuccio, that you will always be drowning yourself in a tumbler of water? Why are you making such a fuss? Don't you know that I take better care of your life than my own? Don't lose courage. Come with me, and you shall see what I can do." So saying, off she flew. The bird alighted in the woods, and as soon as she began to chirp, there came a large flock of birds who settled all about her. She told them the whole story, assuring them that whoever could deprive the sorceress of sight would be protected forever from the talons of the hawks, and the guns and arrows and slingshots of hunters.

Among the birds was a swallow who made her nest against a beam of the royal palace. This swallow hated the sorceress, because several times she had driven the bird away with her nasty-smelling concoctions. Partly out of a desire for revenge, and partly to gain the reward, the swallow offered to perform the service. Away she flew like lightning to the city, and entering the palace, found the sorceress lying on a couch, with two servants fanning her. The swallow came directly over the sorceress and pecked out her eyes. Whereupon the sorceress, seeing night in the middle of the afternoon, knew that the kingdom was all lost. She ran screaming from the royal palace and hid herself in a dark cave, where she knocked her head against the wall, until at last she ended her days.

When the sorceress was gone, Miuccio returned to the King and, following the bird's instructions, said, "I have served you to the best of my ability. The sorceress is blinded, the kingdom is yours. For my reward, I wish only to be left to my own ill fortune, without being again exposed to these dangers."

But the King, embracing him with great affection, told him to sit beside him. The old Queen was enraged at this, Heaven knows. By the rainbow of colors that appeared on her face, one could see the storm that was brewing in her heart against poor Miuccio.

Not far from this castle lived a most ferocious dragon, who was born at the same hour as the Queen. The astrologers had told her father that his daughter would be safe as long as the dragon was safe; when one died, the other would also die. If the Queen happened to die, she could be brought back to life if her temples, chest, nostrils, and wrists were anointed with the blood of the same dragon.

Now the Queen, knowing the strength and fury of this dragon, decided to send Miuccio into his claws. She knew that the beast would make but a mouthful of him, and that he would be like a strawberry swallowed by a bear. So turning to the King, she said, "Upon my word, this Miuccio is the treasure of your house. No wonder you love him, especially since he wants to kill the dragon, who, though he is my brother, is still your enemy. And I care more for one hair on your head than for a hundred brothers."

The King, who hated the dragon mortally, instantly called for Miuccio, and said to him, "I know that you can do whatever you set out to accomplish. Grant me one more pleasure, and then ask for anything you choose. Go this very instant and kill the dragon. You will do me a unique service, and I will reward you well for it."

At these words, Miuccio nearly lost his mind. As soon as he was able to speak, he said to the King, "What a headache you give me by your continual teasing! Is my life only a goatskin rug that you are forever wearing it away by walking all over it? This is not a ripe pear ready to be eaten, but a dragon, that tears with his claws, crushes with his tail, crunches with his teeth, poisons with his eyes, and kills with his breath. Why do you want to send me to death? Is this my reward for having given you a kingdom? What wicked person has taught you these games and put these words into your mouth?"

Then the King grew stubborn. He stamped his feet, and said, "After all you have done, do you fail at the last? No more words. Go, rid my kingdom of this beast, unless you want me to rid you of your life."

Poor Miuccio, who one minute received a favor, another a threat; first a pat on the cheek, and then a kick; now a kind word, then a cruel one! How fleeting and unreliable is the favor of a king. But he knew it would be foolish to answer back, like plucking a lion by the beard. So he withdrew, cursing his fate. And as he was sitting on the doorstep, with his head between his knees, washing his shoes with his tears, the bird came flying with a plant in her beak. Throwing it to him, she said, "Get up, Miuccio, and take courage! Take this plant, and when you come to the cave of that horrid dragon, throw it in. Instantly such a drowsiness will come over him that he will fall fast asleep. Then if you nick and stick him with a big knife, you may soon make an end of him. Then come away, for things will turn out better than you think."

"Enough!" cried Miuccio. "He who has time has life." So saying, he got up, and sticking a pruning knife in his belt and taking the plant, he worked his way up to the dragon's cave, which was under a mountain so high that three other mountains, one on top of the other, would not have reached up to its waist. When he at last reached the entrance to the cave he threw the plant inside. Instantly a deep sleep laid hold of the dragon, and Miuccio began to cut him into pieces.

Now just as he was chopping up the dragon, the old Queen felt a cutting pain at her heart. She called her stepson, the King, and told him what the astrologers had predicted— how her life depended on the dragon, and how she feared that Miuccio had killed him, for she felt herself gradually sliding away.

The King replied, "If you knew that the life of the dragon was the prop of your life, why did you make me send Miuccio? It's your own fault. You have done yourself the mischief, and you must suffer for it."

And the Queen answered, "I never thought that such a boy could have the skill and strength to overthrow a beast who can

The Dragonslayer

make mincemeat of a whole army of men. But since I reckoned wrong, do me one kindness if you love me. When I am dead, take a sponge dipped in the blood of this dragon and anoint all of my limbs before you bury me."

"That is a small thing to ask," replied the King. "And if the blood of the dragon is not enough, I will add my own to give you satisfaction."

The Queen was about to thank him, but the words died upon her breath, for just then Miuccio had made an end of the dragon.

No sooner had Miuccio returned to the castle than the King ordered him to go back for the dragon's blood. Being curious to see the deed done, the King followed him back to the cave. And as Miuccio was going out of the palace gate, the bird met him, and said, "Where are you going?"

Miuccio answered, "I am going where the King sends me. He makes me fly backwards and forwards like a shuttle, and never lets me rest an hour."

"Why are you going?" asked the bird.

"To fetch the blood of the dragon," said Miuccio.

And the bird replied, "Ah, wretched youth! This dragon's blood will cause to spring up again the evil seed of all your misfortunes. The Queen is always exposing you to new dangers. And the King, who lets this odious creature lead him about like a donkey, orders you to endanger your life, which is, in truth, his own flesh and blood. But the wretched man does not know you, although the natural affection he feels for you should have made him realize this. And the services you have done for him should have earned favor for unhappy Porziella,

159

your mother, who for fourteen years has been buried alive in a garret."

While the bird was speaking, the King overheard every word. He stepped forward to learn the truth. Hearing that Miuccio was his own son, and that Porziella was still alive in the garret, he instantly gave orders that she should be set free and brought before him. And when he saw her, looking more beautiful than ever, owing to the care taken by the bird, he embraced her with the greatest affection. He kissed first the mother and then the son, begging forgiveness of Porziella for his ill treatment of her, and begging forgiveness of his son for all the dangers to which he had exposed him. Then he ordered Porziella to be dressed in the finest robes, and had her crowned Queen before all the people. And then the King offered the bird his kingdom and his life. But the bird said her only wish was to have Miuccio for a husband. And as she uttered the words she was changed into a beautiful maiden, and, to the great joy and satisfaction of the King and Porziella, she took Miuccio for her husband. Then the newly married couple went on their way to their own kingdom, where they told everyone that their good fortune was due to the kindness Porziella had shown to the fairy long ago in the woods, for in the end—

A good deed is never lost.

THE TWO CAKES

THERE were once two sisters, named Luceta and Troccola, who had two daughters, Marziella and Puccia. Marziella was as fair to look upon as she was good at heart; while Puccia had a homely face and also a cold heart. But Puccia took after her mother, who likewise was a scarecrow on the outside, and a witch on the inside.

Now it happened that Luceta was boiling some parsnips, in order to fry them with green sauce. She said to her daughter, "Marziella, my dear, go to the well and fetch me a pitcher of water."

"With all my heart, Mother," replied the girl, "but if you love me give me a cake to eat with a drink of the fresh water."

"By all means," said the mother. She took from a basket a beautiful cake (for she had baked a batch the day before), and gave it to Marziella, who set a pitcher on a pad upon her head, and walked to the fountain. And as she stooped down to fill her pitcher, up came a hump-backed old woman; seeing the beautiful cake, she said to Marziella, "My pretty girl, give me a little piece of your cake, and Heaven will send you good fortune!"

Marziella, who was as generous as a queen, replied, "Take it all, my good woman; I am only sorry that it is not made of sugar and almonds."

The Two Cakes

The old woman, seeing Marziella's kindness, said to her, "May Heaven reward you for the goodness you have shown me! I pray that you will always be happy; that when you breathe, roses and jasmine will fall from your mouth; that when you comb your hair, pearls and garnets will fall from it; and when you set your foot on the ground lilies and violets will spring up."

Marziella thanked the old woman, and went on her way home to eat supper with her mother. And the next morning, as Marziella was combing her hair, she saw a shower of pearls and garnets fall from it into her lap. She called her mother with great joy, and they put them all into a basket, and Luceta went to sell some of them in the marketplace. Meanwhile, Troccola came to see her sister, and finding her niece so happy and busy with the pearls, she asked her how she had gotten them. The maiden told her aunt all about meeting the old woman at the fountain. Then Troccola no longer cared to wait for her sister's return, for every hour seemed to her a thousand years until she got home again. There, she quickly gave a cake to her daughter, and sent her for water to the fountain. Puccia found the same old woman. And when the old woman asked her for a little piece of cake, Puccia answered gruffly, "Have I nothing to do but to give you cake? Do you think I am so foolish that I would give you what belongs to me? Charity begins at home, that's what I always say." And so saying, she swallowed the cake in four pieces, making the old woman's mouth water. When she saw the last morsel disappear, she exclaimed in a rage, "Begone! And whenever you breathe, may you foam at the mouth like a mule, may toads drop from your lips, and every time you set foot to the ground may there spring up thorns and thistles!"

Puccia took the pitcher of water and returned home, where her mother was eager to hear what had happened at the fountain. But no sooner did Puccia open her lips, than a shower of toads fell from them. At the sight of the toads, Troccola was furious.

Now, some time later, Marziella's brother, Ciommo, was at the King's court, and the conversation there concerned the beauty of various women. He stepped forward, and said that his sister was the most beautiful woman in the kingdom. When the King heard these praises he told Ciommo to bring his sister to the court, saying that if she was as beautiful as he said he would take her for his wife.

Ciommo immediately sent a messenger to his mother, begging her to come instantly with Marziella. But Luceta, who was not feeling well, commended the lamb to the wolf and begged her sister to take Marziella to the court. Whereupon Troccola, who saw that matters were playing into her hands, promised to take Marziella safe and sound, and then embarked with her niece and Puccia in a boat. When they were some way out at sea, while the sailors were asleep, she threw Marziella into the water. But just as the poor girl was on the point of being drowned there came a most beautiful siren, who took her in her arms and carried her off.

When Troccola arrived at court, Ciommo, who had not seen his sister for a long time, mistook Puccia for her, taking her instantly to the King. But no sooner did Puccia open her lips than toads dropped from them. When the King looked at her more closely he saw that as she breathed she made a lather at her mouth, which looked just like soapsuds. And looking down on the ground, he saw a patch of ugly thorns. Seeing all this he drove Puccia and her mother away, and demoted Ciommo to goosekeeper.

Ciommo, in despair, drove the geese into the fields every day, and let them go their way along the seashore. He slept in into a little straw hut, where he bewailed his lot until it was time to return to court in the evening. But while the geese were running about on the shore, Marziella came out of the sea and fed them with sweet nuts, and give them rosewater to drink, so that the geese grew as big as sheep, and were so fat they could hardly see straight. And every evening, when the geese returned to a little garden under the King's window, they began to sing—

> "Pair, pair, pair!
> The sun and the moon are bright and clear,
> But she who feeds us is still more fair."

Now the King, hearing this goose-music every evening, called Ciommo and asked what he was feeding his geese. And Ciommo replied, "I give them nothing to eat but the fresh grass of the field."

The King was not satisfied with this answer, so he sent a trusty servant to watch Ciommo and see where he drove the geese. The man followed in his footsteps, and saw him go into the little straw shed, leaving the geese to wander along the shore. Then he saw Marziella rise up out of the sea. When the servant of the King saw this, he ran back to his master, beside himself with amazement, and told him about the pretty spectacle he had seen upon the seashore.

The curiosity of the King was aroused by this news, and he wanted to see the beautiful sight for himself. So the next morning, when Ciommo took the geese out, the King followed behind him. And when Ciommo went into the little hut, leaving the geese to wander along the seashore, the King saw Marziella rise out of the water. She gave the geese a trayful of sweet nuts to eat and a cupful of rosewater to drink, then seated herself on a rock and began to comb her locks, from which fell handfuls of pearls and garnets. At the same time, a cloud of flowers dropped from her mouth, and under her feet grew a carpet of lilies and violets.

When the King saw this sight, he called Ciommo and, pointing to Marziella, asked him whether he knew that beautiful maiden. Then Ciommo, recognizing his sister, ran to embrace her. She told them all about the treacherous conduct of her aunt, Troccola, and how that wicked creature had brought her to dwell in the waters of the sea.

The King was overjoyed to find so fair a jewel. He told Ciommo that she was three times more beautiful than he had described her, and she was more than worthy to be his wife, if she would agree.

"Alas, could it be so," answered Marziella. "But can't you see this golden chain upon my foot? When I take too much fresh air, and stay too long on the shore, the siren who saved me from drowning draws me back into the waves; she keeps me held in rich slavery by this golden chain."

"How can I free you from the claws of this siren?" asked the King.

Replied Marziella, "Cut this chain with a smooth file, and loose me from it."

"Wait till morning," answered the King. "I will come with the file, and take you home with me, where you shall be the pupil of my eye, the core of my heart, and the life of my soul."

She shook hands with him to seal their bargain, and went back into the seawater. The King lay awake all night long, thinking about Marziella, the marvels of her hair, the miracles of her mouth, and the wonders at her feet. He chided the sun for not arriving soon enough, so he could bring this treasure home.

While he was all at sea with his dreams, thinking of her who was really in the sea, the sun finally appeared, smoothing the road with his bright rays. Then the King dressed himself, and went with Ciommo to the seashore, where he found Marziella. With his own hand the King used a smooth file to cut the gold chain from the foot of his beloved, but all the while forging a stronger one for his heart. Then, setting her on the saddle behind him, he set out for the royal palace. There, by his command, all the handsome ladies of the land were assembled to receive Marziella as their Queen. There were great festivities at the wedding ceremony. The King ordered that Troccola should be shut up in a tub, and made to suffer for the evil she had shown to Marziella. Then sending for Luceta, he gave her and Ciommo enough to live on like princes. But

The Two Cakes

Puccia was driven out of the kingdom, where she had to beg for her food. This was her reward. Because she did not share a little bit of cake, she now had no bread. For it is said that—

He who shows no pity finds none.

THE SEVEN DOVES

THERE was once in the county of Arzano a good woman who every year gave birth to a son, until at last there were seven of them, who looked like the pipes of the god Pan, with seven reeds, each one larger than another. After they changed their first teeth, they said to Jannetella their mother, "Hark, Mother, if, after so many sons, you do not this time have a daughter, we will leave home, and go wandering through the world like the sons of the blackbirds."

When their mother heard this announcement, she prayed that it should not come to pass, as she did not wish to lose seven such jewels. And when the hour of the birth was at hand, the sons said to Jannetella, "We will climb to the top of yonder hill. If you give birth to a son, put an inkstand and a pen in the window; but if you have a little girl, put up a spoon and a spindle. If we see the signal of a daughter, we shall return home and spend the rest of our lives under your wings. But if we see the signal of a son, then forget us, for we will run away."

Soon after the sons had departed, Jannetella gave birth to a pretty little daughter. She told the nurse to signal the brothers that it was a girl, but the woman was so confused that she put the inkstand and the pen in the window. As soon as the seven brothers saw this signal, they set off, and walked on and on,

169

until at the end of three years they came to a wood, where the trees danced like swords, and the river made music upon the stones. In this wood was the house of an ogre who had been blinded by a woman while he slept. So furious was he with women that he devoured all he could catch.

When the boys arrived at the ogre's house, tired from walking and faint from hunger, they begged him for a morsel of bread. And the ogre replied that if they would serve him he would give them food, and they would only need to watch over him like a dog, each taking turns for one day a week. The youths, upon hearing this, thought they had found a home. They quickly agreed and remained in the service of the ogre. He learned all of their names by heart and gave each one his own room and enough food and money to live on.

Meanwhile, their little sister had grown up. Hearing that her seven brothers, owing to the stupidity of the nurse, had set out to walk through the world, and that no news of them had ever been heard, she felt she must go in search of them. And she begged and pleaded with her mother until at last the good woman gave her permission to go. Then the maiden walked and walked, asking at every place she came to whether anyone had seen seven brothers. She journeyed on, until at last she got news of them at an inn. Told that her brothers were living in the wood, she set out early one morning to find them. She arrived at the ogre's house, where she told her brothers all about the silly nurse. The boys were overjoyed to see her and cursed the inkstand and the pen for writing such misfortune for them. Then giving her a thousand kisses, they told her to remain quiet in their chamber, so that the ogre might not see her—telling her also to give part of her dinner to a cat which was in the room, or otherwise the cat might harm her. Cianna (for so the sister was named) memorized these instructions and shared everything with the cat, like a good companion, always dividing her food equally, saying, "This for me—this for thee —this for the daughter of the King," giving the cat a share to the last morsel.

Now it happened one day that the brothers, going out to hunt food for the ogre, left Cianna a little basket of chickpeas to cook. As she was sorting through them it was her bad luck to find among them a hazel-nut. Accidentally, she swallowed it without giving half to the cat. Out of spite the cat jumped on the table and blew out the candle. Left in darkness, Cianna didn't know what to do. She left the room, disobeying her brothers, and going into the ogre's chamber begged him for a little light. The ogre, hearing a woman's voice, cannily said, "Welcome, madam! You have come to the right place."

And so saying he took a whet stone, and began to sharpen his tusks. But Cianna, who sensed the danger, seized a candle and ran back to her chamber and locked the door, placing against it bars, stools, bedsteads, tables, stones, and everything else there was in the room.

As soon as the ogre had put an edge on his teeth he ran to the brothers' chamber and began kicking at the door to break it open. Hearing the noise and disturbance the seven brothers came home at once, and hearing themselves accused by the ogre of treachery for making their room a refuge for a woman, the eldest brother, who was also the smartest, said to the ogre, "We know nothing about it. Perhaps this wicked woman came into the room while we were out hunting. But as she is locked inside, come with me and I will show you how to seize her."

Then they took the ogre by the hand, and led him to a deep, deep pit, where, giving him a push, they sent him headlong to the bottom. And taking a shovel, they covered him over with earth. Then they told their sister to open the door, and they scolded her soundly for not heeding their warning, and told her to be more careful in the future, and not to pluck any grass upon the spot where the ogre was buried, or they would be turned into seven doves.

"Heaven keep me from bringing such a misfortune upon you!" replied Cianna. So, taking possession of all the ogre's riches, and making themselves masters of the whole house, they lived there merrily enough, waiting for the winter to pass away, and the spring to come, when the sun would give the earth a green gown embroidered with flowers, and they might set out on their journey home.

Now it happened one day, when the brothers had gone to the mountains to get firewood to protect themselves against the winter, which grew colder every day, that a poor traveler came to the ogre's wood, and made faces at a monkey perched up in a pine tree. The monkey became annoyed and threw down large pine cones on the man's head, which made such a terrible bump that the poor man began to cry. Cianna, hearing the noise, went out and, taking pity on his disaster, she quickly plucked a sprig of rosemary from a tuft of grass which grew upon the ogre's grave. She boiled the sprig with flour and salt and made a plaster for his head. After giving the man some breakfast she sent him on his way.

The Seven Doves

While Cianna was preparing dinner and waiting for her brothers to return home, lo! she saw seven doves come flying to her.

"You foolish girl, you have plucked the rosemary from the ogre's grave and brought calamity upon us! Have you the brains of a cat, Sister, that you have forgotten our warning? Now we are turned into doves, prey to the talons of hawks and falcons! Behold us, now we are companions to water-hens, goldfinches, woodpeckers, owls, magpies, jays, rooks, wood-cocks, chickens, turkeys, blackbirds, thrushes, finches, green-finches, crossbills, flycatchers, larks, kingfishers, wagtails, robins, sparrows, ducks, pigeons, and even a goose! Look at what you have done! To heal the head of a wanderer, you have broken the heads of seven brothers. And there is no help for our misfortune, unless you find the Mother of Time, who will tell you the way to get us out of trouble."

Cianna, who was terribly sorry for her mistake, begged her brothers to forgive her, and offered to go around the world until she found the dwelling of the old woman. Then asking them to stay in the house until she returned, so they would be safe, she set out, and journeyed on and on without ever tiring. Though she went on foot, her desire to help her brothers spurred her on. At last she came to the seashore, where the waves were crashing on the rocks. Here she saw a huge whale, who said to her, "My pretty maiden, what go you seeking?"

And she replied, "I am seeking the dwelling of the Mother of Time."

"Hear then what you must do," replied the whale. "Go straight along this shore, and on coming to the first river, follow it up to its source, and you will meet with someone who will show you the way. But do me one favor: when you find the good old woman, beg her to tell me how I may swim about safely, without so often knocking upon the rocks and being thrown up on the sands."

"Trust me," said Cianna. And thanking the whale for his help, she set off walking along the shore. After a long journey she came to the river, which wound its silvery way to the sea. Following it to its source, she arrived at beautiful open country, where the heavenly meadow displayed her green mantle starred over with flowers. There she met a mouse who said to her, "Where are you going all by yourself, my pretty girl?"

And Cianna replied, "I am seeking the Mother of Time."

"You have a long way to go," said the mouse. "But do not lose heart, everything has an end. Walk on toward those mountains, which, like the lords of these fields, are called Majesty, and you will learn more news. But do me one favor: when you arrive at the house you are looking for, ask the good old woman to tell us how to escape the tyranny of the cats. Then I will be your servant."

Cianna, after promising to do the mouse this kindness, set off towards the mountains, which, although they appeared to be nearby, seemed never to be reached. When she came to them at last, she sat down upon a large stone; and there she saw an army of ants, carrying a store of grain. One of the busy ants turned to Cianna and said, "Who are you, and where are you going?"

And Cianna, who was courteous to everyone, said, "I am

Lise in the Snow with the Casket
Page 184

Nannillo and Nennella in the Wood
Page 203

While Cianna was preparing dinner, seven white doves flew onto the windowsill.

an unhappy girl, who is seeking the dwelling of the Mother of Time."

"Go on farther," said the ant, "and where these mountains open into a large plain you will obtain more news. But do me a great favor: ask the old woman what we ants can do to live a little longer. For it seems to me a folly to be heaping up so much food for so short a life."

"Ease your mind," said Cianna. "I will return the kindness you have shown me."

Then she crossed the mountains and arrived at a wide plain. And proceeding a little way over it, she came to a large oak tree, a memorial of antiquity, whose acorns had lost all their sweetness. Then the oak, making lips of its bark and a tongue of its core, said to Cianna, "Where are you going, my little daughter? Come and rest under my shade."

Cianna thanked him, but excused herself, saying that she was hurrying to find the Mother of Time. When the oak heard this, he replied, "You are not far from her dwelling. Before you have gone another day's journey, you will see a house upon a mountain. There you will find her whom you seek. But if you have as much kindness as beauty, let me ask you to learn what I can do to regain my lost honor. For instead of providing food for great men, I now only provide food for hogs."

"Leave it to me," replied Cianna. "I will take care to serve you." So saying, she departed, and walked on and on without ever resting. She came at last to the foot of a mountain, which was poking its head into the clouds. There she found a tired old man who had lain down upon some hay. Cianna recognized him as the traveler she had aided, and the old man remembered her and the help she had given him.

When the old man heard who she was seeking, he told her that he was carrying to Time himself the rent for his farm, and that Time was a tyrant who took everything for himself and claimed tribute from everyone, especially from people of his age. Cianna had been so kind to him, he would repay her by giving her some good information about her destination. He was sorry he could not accompany her there, but his old age obliged him to remain at the foot of those mountains, to settle up his accounts with the clerks of Time, which are the labors, suffering, and infirmities of life. In that way do the old pay their debts to Nature. So the old man said to her, "Now, my pretty, innocent child, listen to me. On the top of this mountain you will find a ruined house, which was built long ago. The walls are cracked, the foundations crumbling away, the doors worm-eaten, the furniture all worn out—in short, everything is gone to wrack and ruin. On one side are shattered columns, on another broken statues. Nothing is in good condition except a coat-of-arms over the door, bearing a serpent biting its tail, a stag, a raven, and a phoenix.

"Inside the house are files, saws, pruning hooks, scythes, and hundreds and hundreds of big jars full of ashes. Written on the jars are the names of Corinth, Carthage, Troy, and a thousand other cities, the ashes of which Time has kept as trophies of his conquests.

"When you come near the house, hide yourself and wait until Time goes out. As soon as he has gone, enter, and you will find an old, old woman, with a beard that touches the ground and a hump reaching to the sky. Her hair, like the tail of a dapple-gray horse, covers her heels. Her face looks like a pleated collar, with the folds stiffened by the starch of years. The old woman sits on top of a clock, hanging on a wall. Her eyebrows are so large that they hang over her eyes, so that she will not be able to see you. As soon as you enter, quickly take the pendulum off the clock. Then call to the old woman, and beg her to answer your questions. She will instantly call her son to come and eat you up, but the clock upon which the old woman sits will have lost its weights, and her son will not be able to move. She will be forced to tell you what you wish. But do not trust any oath she may make, unless she swears by the wings of her son."

So saying, the poor old man fell down and crumbled away, like an old dead body brought out of a catacomb into the light of day. Then Cianna took his ashes and mixed them with a pint of her tears. She made a grave and buried them, praying that Heaven would grant them peace.

Then she climbed the mountain till she was quite out of breath, and waited until Time came out. He was an old man with a long, long beard, and he wore a very old cloak covered with slips of paper, on which were written the names of various people. He had large wings, and ran so fast that he was out of sight in an instant.

When Cianna entered the house of his mother, she instantly seized the weights of the clock and begged the old woman to answer her questions. The old Mother of Time set up a loud cry, calling to her son. But Cianna said to her, "You may butt your head against the wall as long as you like, for you will not see your son while I hold these clock weights."

The old woman, seeing that she was defeated, began to coax Cianna, saying, "Let go of them, my dear, and do not stop my son's course; for no person living has ever done that. Let go of the clock weights, and I promise you that I will do you no harm."

Answered Cianna, "You must say something better than that if you would have me loosen my grip."

"I swear to you by those teeth which gnaw all mortal things that I will tell you all you desire."

"That means nothing," answered Cianna, "for I know you are deceiving me."

"Well, then," said the old woman, "I swear to you by those heavenly wings which fly over everyone that I will give you more pleasure than you imagine."

And so, Cianna let go of the weights and kissed the old woman's hand, which felt moldy and smelled quite bad. The old woman, seeing the courtesy of the young woman, said to her, "Hide yourself behind this door, and when Time comes home I will make him tell me all you wish to know. And as soon as he goes out again—for he never stays long in one place —you can leave. But do not let him see you or hear you, for he is such a glutton that he does not spare even his own children. When all fails, he devours himself and then springs up anew."

Cianna did as the old woman told her. And, soon after, Time came flying in, having gnawed whatever came to hand, down to the very mold on the walls. He was about to leave again, when his mother asked him all the questions she had heard from Cianna. She begged him to answer exactly, and after a thousand entreaties, her son replied: "To the tree may be answered, that it can never be prized by men so long as it keeps treasures buried under its roots. To the mice, that they will never be safe from the cat unless they tie a bell to her leg to tell them when she is coming. To the ants, that they will live a hundred years if they can stop flying, for when the ant is going to die she grows wings. To the whale, that it should be of good cheer, and make friends with the sea-mouse, who will act as a guide, so that he will always go in the right direction. And to the doves, that when they alight on the column of wealth, they will return to their former state."

So saying, Time set out to run his accustomed posts. Cianna said goodbye to the old woman, and climbed down to the foot of the mountain, just as the seven doves, who had followed their sister's footsteps, arrived there. Wearied with flying so far, they stopped to rest upon the horn of a dead ox. No sooner had they alighted than they were changed back into handsome youths just as they had been before. But while they were marvelling at this, they heard the reply which Time had given, and saw at once that the column where they rested was a symbol of the horn of plenty, the column of wealth of which Time had spoken. They embraced their sister with great joy, and all set out, going back on the same road by which Cianna had come. When they came to the oak tree, and told it what Cianna had heard from Time, the tree begged them to take away the treasure from its roots, since it was the cause of its acorns having turned bitter. The seven brothers took a spade which they found in a garden, and dug and dug, until they

The Seven Doves

came to a great heap of gold money, which they divided into eight parts and shared with their sister, so that they might carry it away. But being wearied with the journey and the heavy load, they laid themselves down to sleep under a hedge. Soon a band of robbers came by, and seeing the poor fellows asleep, with their heads upon the clothfuls of money, tied them hand and foot to some trees and took away their money, leaving them without their wealth, which had slipped through their fingers as soon as they had found it.

As they were lamenting their unhappy fate, up came the mouse, who, as soon as she heard the reply which Time had given, nibbled the cords which bound them and set them free.

Having gone a little way farther, they met the ant, who, when she heard the advice of Time, asked Cianna why she was so pale-faced and sad. And when Cianna told her their misfortune, and the trick which the robbers had played on them, the ant replied, "Now I can return the kindness you have done me. While I was carrying a load of grain underground, I saw a place where these thieves hide their loot. They have dug a hole underneath an old building, in which they shut up all the things they have stolen. Right now they are carrying out some new robbery; I will go with you and show you the place, so that you may recover your money."

So saying, she led them toward some tumbled-down houses, and showed them the opening to the pit. The eldest brother, who was bolder than the others, entered and found there all of their money.

Then taking their treasure with them, they walked on toward the seashore, where they found the whale, and told him the good advice which Time had given them. And while they stood talking, they saw the robbers suddenly appear, armed to the teeth. At the sight they exclaimed, "Alas, alas! We are lost, for here come the robbers armed with knives to skin us alive!"

"Don't be afraid," replied the whale, "for I can save you, and will so repay the love you have shown me. Climb upon my back, and I will quickly carry you to safety."

Cianna and her brothers, seeing the enemy at their heels and the water up to their throats, climbed upon the whale, who, keeping far away from the rocks, carried them to within sight of Naples. But being afraid to take them ashore on account of the shallow harbor, he said, "Where would you like me to land you? On the shore of Amalfi?"

The eldest brother answered, "I'd rather not, my dear fish. I do not wish to land at any place hereabouts. At Massa they are too snooty. At Sorrento there are too many thieves. At Vico they send you on your way. And at Castel-a-mare no one even says hello."

Then the whale, to please them, turned around and swam toward the Salt Rock, where he left them. From there, they were picked up by the first fishing boat that passed, and returned to their own country, safe and sound and rich, to the great joy of their mother. And, thanks to the goodness of Cianna, they enjoyed a happy life, proving the old saying—

Do good whenever you can, and forget it.

LISE AND THE MAGIC BOX

ONCE upon a time there were two brothers—Cianne, who was as rich as a lord, and Lise, who had barely enough to live on. But poor as one was in fortune, the other was poor in heart, and he would not give his brother a penny even to save his life. Poor Lise, in despair, left his country, and set out to wander over the world. He wandered on and on, till one wet and cold evening he came to an inn, where he found twelve young men sitting around a fire. When they saw poor Lise numb with cold, because his clothes were nothing but rags, they invited him to sit down by the fire.

Lise accepted the invitation and began to warm himself. Then, one young man, whose face was a picture of gloom, said to him, "What do you think of this weather?"

"What do I think of it?" replied Lise. "I think that all the months of the year serve a purpose; but we don't know what we want. In winter, when it rains, we want the sun, and in the month of August we want the rain; without thinking that if that were the case the seasons would be turned upside-down, the seed sown would be lost, the crops would be destroyed, and Nature would go head over heels. So, let's leave Heaven to its own course; for it has made the tree to ease the winter's cold with its wood, and with its leaves relieve the heat of summer."

183

Lise and the Magic Box

"You speak like a wise man!" replied the youth. "But you cannot deny that this month of March, which we are now in, is not pleasant, with all this frost and rain, snow and hail, wind and storm, these fogs and other troubles, that make one's life a burden."

"You only speak about the bad things of March," replied Lise, "but you don't mention the benefits it brings. By introducing the spring, it begins the production of things, and leads the sun into the house of the Ram."

The youth was greatly pleased at what Lise said, for he was in fact the month of March itself, who had arrived at that inn with his eleven brothers. To reward Lise's goodness, since he had not found anything bad to say of a month so sad that shepherds won't mention it, he gave him a beautiful little casket, saying, "Take this, and if you want anything, only ask for it, and when you open this box you will see it before you."

Lise thanked the youth, and laying the little box under his head instead of a pillow, he went to sleep.

All through the night it snowed and snowed, till the whole country lay under a thick white blanket. As soon as the sun touched the horizon, Lise said goodbye to the young men and set out on his way. But he had hardly gone fifty steps from the inn, when he sank to his knees in the snow. Opening the casket, he said, "Ah, my friend, I wish I had a sleigh lined with fur so that I might travel warm and comfortable through the snow!"

No sooner had he uttered the words than there appeared a sleigh with horses, and a driver with a fur lap robe who tucked him in all comfortable and warm and drove him on to the next resting place.

When he arrived at the inn it was late at night and there was nothing to eat. Being hungry, Lise opened the little box and said, "I wish for something to eat." And instantly there appeared a selection of the choicest food, and there was such a banquet that ten kings might have feasted on it.

One evening, when he came to a forest which was leafy and overgrown, Lise opened the little casket, and said, "I should like to rest tonight on this beautiful spot, where the river is making music over the stones to accompany the song of the cool breezes."

And instantly there appeared, under a tent, a scarlet sofa, with down mattresses, covered with damask and silk sheets as light as a feather. Then he asked for something to eat, and there appeared a table covered with silver and gold fit for a prince, and another table spread with the most delectable dishes that even a king's chef couldn't imagine.

When he had eaten enough, he laid himself down to sleep. When he awoke, Lise opened his little box and said, "I wish to dress handsomely, for today I shall return home to see my brother, and I should like to make his mouth water."

No sooner said than done: immediately a princely outfit of the richest black velvet appeared, with edgings of plush red wool and a lining of yellow silk embroidered all over with field of flowers. So, getting dressed, Lise mounted one of his horses and rode on to his brother's house.

When Cianne saw his brother arrive, with all this splendor and luxury, he wished to know what good fortune had

Lise and the Magic Box

befallen him. Lise told him of the young men whom he had met in the inn, and of the present they had made him; but he did not tell him about the magic powers of the box.

Cianne was now impatient to get away from his brother, and go to the inn himself. He told Lise to go and rest, as he was tired. Then he started right away, and soon arrived at the inn, where, finding the same young men, he fell into conversation with them. And when the youth asked him the same question, what he thought of that month of March, Cianne, being a mean-spirited person, said, "It is a miserable month! A month of which nothing good can be said. A month of which, when you want to call a man a nuisance, you say, 'He looks like March to me.' In short, it is a month so hateful, that it would be the best fortune for the world, the greatest blessing to the earth, the greatest gain to men, if it would be excluded from the band of twelve brothers."

March, who heard himself so maligned, suppressed his anger till the morning, intending at that time to reward Cianne for his nasty talk. And when Cianne was ready to leave, he gave him a fine whip, saying to him, "Whenever you wish for anything, only say, 'Whip, give me a hundred!' And you shall receive what you deserve."

Cianne, thanking the youth, went off quickly, not wanting to try the whip until he reached home. As soon as he set foot in the house, he went into a secret room, intending to hide the money which he expected to receive from the whip. Then he said, "Whip, give me a hundred!"

Instantly, the whip began to strike him everywhere—on his legs, his back, his head, arms and chest. And each stroke

Lise and the Magic Box

was given in earnest, so that Lise, hearing his cries, came running to the room. When Lise saw that the whip, like a runaway horse, could not stop itself, he opened the little box and brought it to a standstill. Then he asked Cianne what had happened. Hearing his story, he told him he had no one to blame but himself; for like a blockhead he alone had caused his own misfortune, for if he had spoken well of the young men, he might have had the same good reward. To speak well of someone costs nothing, and usually brings an unexpected profit. Lise comforted him, and asked that he not seek more wealth than Heaven had already given him, for Lise's little casket could fill the houses of thirty misers, and Cianne should be master of all he possessed, since to the generous man, heaven is generous. Although another man might have held a grudge against Cianne for his past cruelty, Lise thought that his brother's meanness to him had been a favorable wind which had brought him good fortune, so he was grateful to him.

When Cianne heard these words, he begged his brother's forgiveness, and entering into partnership they enjoyed together their good fortune, and from that time forward Cianne spoke well of everything and everyone, no matter how bad they might be; for—

The dog that was scalded with hot water
forever afterwards fears water which is cold.

THE SUGAR-CANDY PRINCE

A MERCHANT once had an only daughter, whom he wished to see married. But as she would never consent, the father was the most unhappy and miserable man in the world. Now it happened one day that he was going to a fair; so he asked his daughter, who was named Betta, what she would like him to bring her on his return. And she said, "Papa, if you love me, bring me fifty pounds of Palermo sugar, and the same amount of sweet almonds, with four to six bottles of rosewater, and a little musk and amber, also forty pearls, two sapphires, a few garnets and rubies, with some gold thread, and above all a pot and a little silver trowel." Her father wondered at this extravagant demand, but he would not refuse her. Off he went to the fair, and brought back all that she had asked for.

As soon as Betta received these things, she shut herself up in a room, and began to make paste from the almonds and sugar, mixed with rosewater and perfumes. From the paste, she created a beautiful young man, with hair of gold thread, eyes of sapphires, teeth of pearls, and lips of rubies. She gave him such grace that all he needed was a voice. When she had done all this, she prayed to the goddess of Love that the statue should come to life. As she increased her prayers, the statue began to breathe; and after breathing, words began to come; and at last, the statue began to walk.

The Sugar-Candy Prince

With a joy far greater than if she had gained a kingdom, Betta embraced and kissed the man she had created and, taking him by the hand, she led him before her father and said, "My father, you have always wished to see me married, and to please you I have now chosen a husband after my own heart."

When her father saw the handsome youth come out of his daughter's room, he stood amazed. He consented immediately to the marriage. So a great feast was made, at which, among the other ladies present, there appeared an unknown Queen. Seeing the beauty of Pintosmalto (for that was the name Betta gave him), this Queen fell desperately in love with him. Now Pintosmalto, who had only opened his eyes on the world three hours before was as innocent of evil as a newborn baby. Betta had told him to be polite to the guests and when the Queen took him by the hand he followed along out of courtesy. She led him quietly to her coach, drawn by six horses, which stood in the courtyard and then taking him into it, she ordered the coachman to drive off and away to her kingdom.

After Betta waited a while in vain expecting Pintosmalto to return, she sent down into the courtyard to see if he were speaking with anyone there; then she went up to the roof to see if he had gone to take fresh air. But she found him nowhere and she realized that, on account of his great beauty, he had been stolen from her. She made a missing-person's bulletin and posted a reward, but there was no reply. And so she decided to go in search of Pintosmalto herself, even if she should have to search the world over.

Dressing herself as a poor girl, she set out on her way. After some months she came to the house of a good old woman,

The Sugar-Candy Prince

who received her with great kindness. And when she had heard Betta's misfortune, she took pity on her, and taught her three sayings. The first was, "Tricche valicche, the house rains!" The second, "Anola tranola, the fountain plays!" The third, "Scatola matola, the sun shines!" She told Betta to repeat these words whenever she was in trouble, and they would help her.

Betta wondered at this silliness, but thought to herself, "There is some reason for everything in this world and who knows what good fortune may be contained in these words?" So saying, she thanked the old woman, and set out again upon her journey.

After a long trek she came to a beautiful city called Round Mount, where she went straight to the royal palace, and begged for a little shelter in the stable. The ladies of the court ordered a small room to be given her on the stairs; and while poor Betta was sitting there she saw Pintosmalto pass by. She almost fainted from joy, but she didn't dare call out or make herself known because she didn't know what her situation might be. Instead, she decided to use the first saying which the old woman had told her. No sooner had she repeated the words, "Tricche valicche, the house rains!" than instantly there appeared before her a beautiful little coach of gold set all over with jewels, which ran about the room by itself and was a wonder to behold.

When the ladies of the court saw this sight they went and told the Queen, who immediately ran to Betta's room. When she saw the beautiful little coach, she asked whether she would sell it, and offered to pay whatever she might demand. Betta

191

replied that, although she was poor, she would not sell it for all the gold in the world, but if the Queen really wanted the little coach, she must let Betta spend one night at the door of Pintosmalto's room.

The Queen was amazed at the folly of the poor girl, who although she was all in rags would give up riches for a mere whim. She decided to give Pintosmalto a sleeping pill and to let the poor girl spend the night at his door. Pintosmalto would be so fast asleep he wouldn't even know Betta was there.

As soon as night came, the Queen gave a sleeping pill to Pintosmalto, who did everything he was told, and she sent him to bed. No sooner had he laid down on the mattress than he fell sound asleep. Poor Betta, who expected to tell him all her past troubles, had no audience. She cried at his door all night long, but the sleeping Pintosmalto never opened his eyes until the sun appeared. The Queen came down, and taking Pintosmalto by the hand, said to Betta, "Now be content."

"May you have such content all the days of your life!" whispered Betta under her breath. "For I have passed a night so bad that I shall not soon forget it."

The poor girl, however, decided to try the second saying. So she repeated the words, "Anola tranola, the fountain plays!" and instantly there appeared a golden cage, with a beautiful bird made of precious stones and gold, which sang like a nightingale. When the ladies saw this they told the Queen, who wished to see the bird. Then she asked the same question as she had about the little coach, and Betta made the same reply as before. So the Queen, who thought Betta was a very silly girl, promised to grant her wish and took the cage with the bird.

The Sugar-Candy Prince

As soon as night came, the Queen gave Pintosmalto another sleeping pill, and sent him to bed. When Betta saw that he slept like a dead person, she began once more to wail aloud, and so she passed another night, full of trouble, weeping and wailing and tearing her hair. But as soon as day broke the Queen came to fetch her captive, and left poor Betta in grief and sorrow, and biting her nails at the trick that had once again been played on her.

In the morning when Pintosmalto went to a garden outside the city gate to pick some figs, he met a cobbler, who lived in a room close to where Betta stayed and had heard every word she had said. Then he told Pintosmalto of the weeping and crying of the unhappy beggar-girl. Now, Pintosmalto had already begun to get a little more sense, and when he heard this, he guessed how matters stood. He decided that if the same thing happened again, he would not swallow the pill the Queen gave him.

Betta decided finally to try one more time, so she said the words, "Scatola matola, the sun shines!" and instantly there appeared a vast array of fabrics in silk and gold, and embroidered scarves, with a golden cup. The Queen herself could not have brought together so many beautiful ornaments. When the ladies saw these things they told their mistress, who once more asked Betta if she could buy them. But Betta replied as before, that if the Queen wished to have them she must let her spend the night at the door of the room. Then the Queen said to herself, "What can I lose by satisfying this silly girl, in order to get these beautiful things?" So taking all the treasures which Betta offered, as soon as night fell, the Queen gave a third sleeping pill to Pintosmalto. But this time, he did not swallow it, but hid it under his tongue. When the Queen had left his room, he spit out the pill, and and then went to bed.

Betta now began to cry the same tune again, saying how she had made him with her own hands, how she had shaped his body from sugar and almonds, made his hair of gold, and his eyes and mouth of pearls and precious stones, and how the gods had answered her prayers and given him life, and lastly how he had been stolen from her, and how with great difficulty she had gone seeking him. Then she went on to tell him how she had watched two nights at the door of his room, and to do this had given up two treasures, and yet had not heard a single word from him. This was the last night of her hopes and the end of her life.

When Pintosmalto heard these words, he remembered like a dream all that had happened, and he rose and embraced her. Then he went very quietly into the room of the Queen, who was in a deep sleep, and took away all the things that she had taken from Betta, and all her jewels and money to repay Betta for her past troubles. Then he returned to Betta, and they set off and traveled on and on until they arrived at her father's house, where they found him alive and well. From the joy of seeing his daughter again he felt like a young man again. And when the Queen woke up to find them gone, and all her treasures missing, she tore her hair and her clothes, and called to mind the saying—

He who cheats must not complain if he is cheated.

THE SUN, THE MOON, AND TALIA

THERE was once a great Knight, who had a daughter named Talia. And he called on the fortune-tellers and wise men of his kingdom to come and tell him her future. After various discussions they came to the conclusion that a great peril awaited her from a piece of stalk in some flax. Now, flax was a very common plant that was used around the palace by old ladies who spun thread from its fibers; and from the thread other old ladies wove fabric. And so the Knight issued a command, prohibiting any flax to be brought into his house, hoping to avoid the danger.

When Talia was grown up, and was standing one day at the window, she saw an old woman pass by who was carrying a distaff full of dried flax and a spindle full of thread. She had never seen such interesting sticks and she was fascinated to watch as the old woman stopped and twisted and twirled the flax off the distaff stick and spun it into thread that curled around the spindle. Her curiosity was so great that she made the old woman come upstairs. Then, taking the distaff in her hand, Talia began to draw off the flax, when a piece of stalk caught under her fingernail and she fell dead upon the ground. When the old woman saw what had happened, she hobbled downstairs as quickly as she could.

When the unhappy father heard of Talia's death, he wept

The Sun, the Moon, and Talia

bitterly, and placed her in a palace in the country, upon a velvet seat under a canopy of brocade; and locking the doors, he left forever, and tried to forget he had ever been there.

Now, a certain King went hunting one day, and a falcon that he had trained to seek game for him flew off his resting perch and straight to the window of that palace. When the bird did not return at the King's call, he ordered his attendants to knock at the door. After they had knocked for some time, the King ordered them to fetch a ladder, thinking he would climb up and see what was inside. Then he mounted the ladder, and going through the whole palace, he was surprised that there was not a living person in that whole big house. At last he came to the room where Talia was lying, as if enchanted. And when the King saw her, he called to her, thinking that she was asleep, but he called in vain, for she slept on, no matter how loudly he called. So, after admiring her beauty, the King returned home to his kingdom.

Meanwhile, two little twins, one a boy and the other a girl, who looked like two little jewels, wandered into the palace and found Talia in her trance. At first they were afraid because they tried without success to awaken her. But, becoming bolder, the little girl gently took Talia's finger into her mouth, to bite it and so wake her up. And so in this way the splinter of flax popped out of Talia's finger. Immediately, Talia began to awake as from a deep sleep; and when she saw those little jewels at her side, she took them to her heart, and loved them greatly. Yet she wondered how food and refreshment appeared, as if brought by unseen hands.

After a time the King, recalling the beautiful, sleeping

196

maiden went to visit her. When he found her awakened, and with two beautiful little children by her side, he was delighted. The King told Talia who he was, and they formed a great friendship, and he remained there for several days, promising, as he took leave, to return and fetch her.

When the King went back to his own kingdom he was always talking about Talia and the little ones—so much so that when he was eating he had the words Talia on his tongue, and Sun and Moon (for so he named the children) in his mouth. And even when he went to sleep he did not stop speaking of them, first one and then the other.

Now, the King's stepmother had grown suspicious at his long absence, and when she heard him calling Talia, Sun, and Moon, she became angry, and said to the King's secretary, "Tell me who it is that my stepson speaks of, and I will make you rich; but if you lie to me, I'll make you sorry."

The man, moved on the one hand by fear, and on the other by greed, told the Queen the whole truth. And so she sent the secretary in the King's name to Talia, saying that he wished to see the children. Talia happily sent them, but when they arrived the Queen commanded her guard to kill them.

Now the guard, who had a tender heart, seeing the two pretty little children, took compassion on them, and gave them to his wife to keep. Then he killed two goats and told the Queen they were the children.

Meanwhile the Queen was not satisfied with what she had done. She called the secretary again, and sent him to fetch Talia, pretending that the King wished to see her. At this summons Talia went that very instant, longing to see him. But

The Sun, the Moon, and Talia

when she came before the her, the Queen, with a poisonous look, asked, "Are you the pretty mischief-maker? Are you the weed that has caught my son's eye and given me all this trouble?"

When Talia heard this she began to excuse herself; but the Queen would not listen to a word. She had a large bonfire lit in the courtyard, she commanded that Talia should be thrown into the flames. Poor Talia fell on her knees before the Queen and begged her at least to allow her time to take the clothes off her back. The Queen, not so much out of pity for the unhappy girl, as to get hold of her fine dress, which was embroidered all over with gold and pearls, said to her, "Undress yourself—I allow you."

Then Talia began to undress, and as she took off each garment she sighed. When she had stripped off her cloak, her gown, and her jacket, and was about to take off her petticoat, they seized her and were dragging her away. At that moment, the King came up, and demanded to know the whole truth. When he asked also for the children, and heard that his stepmother had ordered them to be killed, the unhappy King was enraged.

He ordered the Queen to be thrown into the same fire, and the secretary along with her. He was going to do the same with the guard, thinking that he had killed the children; but the guard threw himself at the King's feet and said, "Truly, sir King, I wish no other reward for the service I have done you than to be thrown into a furnace full of live coals; I ask no gratitude other than a spike in my heart; no other pleasure than to be roasted in the fire; no other privilege than to have my ashes mingle with those of a Queen. But I ask for nothing as a reward for having saved the children, and brought them back to you in spite of that wicked creature who wished to kill them."

When the King heard these words he was quite beside himself; he could not believe his ears. He said to the guard, "If what you say is true, I will take you from the fire, and reward you so that you shall be the happiest man in the world."

As the King was speaking these words, the guard's wife, seeing her husband's dilemma, quickly brought Sun and Moon before the King. He was so delighted that he turned round and round, kissing first one and then another. Then giving the guard a large reward, he took Talia for his wife. She enjoyed a long life with her husband and the two children, proving that—

> *She who has luck can go to bed,*
> *And bliss will rain upon her head.*

NENNILLO AND NENNELLA

THERE was once a good man named Jannuccio, who had two children, Nennillo and Nennella, whom he loved as much as his own life. But after his wife died, he married a cruel woman, who had no sooner set foot in his house than she began to ride the high horse, saying, "Am I come here indeed to look after other folks' children? A pretty job I have undertaken, to have all this trouble and be constantly teased by a couple of squalling brats! I wish that I had broken my neck instead of coming here to eat bad food, worse drink, and get no sleep at night! What a life I lead! I came as a wife, not as a servant. I must find some means of getting rid of these creatures. I'm done taking care of them. Either they go, or I go."

The poor husband, who liked this new wife a little, said to her, "Softly, Wife! Don't be angry. And tomorrow morning, before the cock crows, I will remove this annoyance in order to please you."

So the next morning, before sunrise, Jannuccio took the children, one by each hand, and with a good basketful of things to eat upon his arm, he led them into the forest, where an army of poplars and beech trees held the shadows captive. Then Jannuccio said, "My little children, stay here in the woods, and eat and drink merrily. If you want anything, follow

201

the line of ashes which I dropped as we came along. This will lead you out of the woods and bring you straight home." Then giving them both a kiss, he returned weeping to his house.

As night began to fall and the shadowy forest grew darker and darker, the two little children began to feel afraid in that lonesome place, where the sound of the river thrashing against the rocks would have frightened even a hero. So they went slowly along the path of ashes, and it was already midnight when they reached their home. When Pascozza, their step-mother, saw the children, she acted like a perfect fury, crying aloud, wringing her hands, stamping her feet, snorting like a frightened horse, and exclaiming, "What fine piece of work is this? Is there no way to get rid of these creatures? Is it possible, Husband, that you are determined to keep them here to make me suffer? Go, take them out of my sight! I'll not wait for the crowing of the cocks and the cackling of the hens. Take them away now, or else tomorrow morning I'll go back to my parents' house, for you do not deserve me. I did not bring you so much fine furniture and so many fine cows, only to be made a slave to children who are not my own."

Poor Jannuccio, who saw that matters were heating up, immediately took the little ones and returned to the forest. He gave the children another basketful of food, and he said to them, "You see, my dears, how this wife of mine—who is your ruin and a nail in my heart—hates you. You must remain in these woods, where the compassionate trees will shelter you from the hot sun, the charitable river will give you fresh, clean water, and the kind earth will give give you a safe pillow of grass. And when you want food, follow this little path of rice which I have dropped in a straight line, and you can seek what you need." So saying, he turned away his face, so the children would not see him weep.

When Nennillo and Nennella had eaten everything in the basket, they wanted to return home. But, alas! A donkey had eaten up all the rice that their father had dropped on the ground. They lost their way, and wandered about forlorn in the woods for several days, eating acorns and chestnuts which they found on the ground. But as Heaven always protects the innocent, there came by chance a Prince out hunting in the woods. Nennillo, hearing the baying of his hunting dogs, was so frightened that he crept into a hollow tree; and Nennella set off running at full speed, and ran until she came out of the forest, and found herself on the seashore. Now it happened that some pirates had landed there to gather up wood. They caught Nennella and carried her off; and their captain took her home with him, where he and his wife, having just lost a little girl, treated her as their daughter.

In the meantime, Nennillo, who had hidden himself in the tree, was surrounded by the furiously barking dogs; when the Prince came and discovered the little boy, he ordered one of the huntsmen to set him upon his saddle and take him to the royal palace. There Nennillo was brought up with great care, and taught many arts and skills. Among others, he learned the skill of carving up sides of beef, whole deer, and every type of game, which in those days, if you remember, was a very high art indeed. Before three or four years had passed, Nennillo became so expert in his art that he could carve a chicken as small as a flea, or a goat as big as an elephant.

Nennillo and Nennella

Now about this time the pirate captain who had taken Nennella to his house was about to be arrested and put on trial for robbery on the high seas. Before the constable could get to his house, to take him prisoner, he fled with all his family in a small boat. No sooner was he upon the open sea than a furious storm blew up, upsetting the boat. Everyone on board was drowned—all except Nennella who, because she was an innocent child, escaped the danger. Just then a large enchanted fish, which was swimming around the capsized boat, opened its huge throat and swallowed her down.

The little girl now thought that her days were surely ended. But suddenly she found inside the fish an amazing sight —beautiful fields and fine gardens, and a splendid mansion, with all that she could desire. There she lived like a princess. The fish carried her to a rock, where the Prince had come to get away from the burning heat of summer and enjoy the cool sea breezes, bringing Nennillo with him. While a banquet was being prepared, Nennillo stepped out upon the rock to sharpen his knives, priding himself greatly on the skills of his job as the Prince's head carver. When Nennella saw him through the fish's throat, she cried aloud,

> "Brother, Brother, your job is done,
> The tables are set out every one;
> But here in the fish I must sit and sigh,
> O brother, without you, I soon shall die."

Nennillo at first paid no attention to the voice, but the Prince heard it and turned toward the sound. He saw the fish;

and when he again heard the same words, he was beside himself with amazement. He ordered his servants to try to catch the fish and draw it to land. They threw a net around it and slowly brought it up to the rock.

Hearing the words "Brother, Brother!" continually repeated, he asked all his servants whether any of them had lost a sister. And Nennillo replied that he barely remembered once having had a sister when the Prince found him in the forest, but that he had never heard any news of her. The Prince told him to get closer to the fish, and see what was the matter, for perhaps this adventure might concern him. As soon as Nennillo approached the fish, it raised up its head, and when it opened its throat Nennella stepped out, so beautiful that she looked just like a nymph appearing as if by magic. And when the Prince asked her how it had all happened, she told him about the wicked stepmother. But she couldn't remember her father's name nor the name of their home. The Prince issued a proclamation, commanding that anyone who had lost two children, named Nennillo and Nennella, should come to the royal palace.

All these years, Jannuccio had passed a sad and unhappy life, believing that his children had been eaten up by wolves. Now he quickly went with the greatest joy to find the Prince, and tell him that he had lost the children. And when he told the story of how he had taken them to the forest, the Prince scolded, calling him a blockhead for allowing his wife to make him send away two such jewels as his children. But after he had broken Jannuccio's head with his words, he applied a soothing bandage by showing him the children. The father embraced them and kissed them for half an hour. Then the Prince sent for Jannuccio's wife and showed her those two golden children all grown up.

"What do you think should be done to someone who would harm these beautiful children?" he asked. "For my part," she replied, "I would put her into a barrel and send her rolling down a mountain."

"It shall be done!" said the Prince. "The goat has butted at herself. Quick now! You have passed the sentence, and you must suffer it."

So he gave orders that the sentence should be instantly carried out.

Then the King chose a very rich knight to be Nennella's husband, and the daughter of another great knight to be Nennillo's bride. He gave them plenty of money to live on, so that they wanted for nothing in the world. But the stepmother, shut into the barrel, and shut out from life, kept on crying through the airhole—

> *"To him who seeks mischief, mischief shall fall;*
> *There comes an hour that repays all."*